GHOST ON THE LOOSE!

Helen Dunwoodie

Galaxy

CHIVERS PRESS
BATH

First published 1998
by
Corgi Yearling
This Large Print edition published by
Chivers Press
by arrangement with
Transworld Publishers Ltd
2002

ISBN 0 7540 7830 2

British Library Cataloguing in Publication Data.

Dunwoodie, Helen
  Ghost on the loose!.—Large print ed.
  1. Ghost stories 2. Children's stories
  3. Large type books
  I. Title
  823. 9'14[J]

ISBN 0-7540-7830-2

Printed and bound in Great Britain by
BOOKCRAFT, Midsomer Norton, Somerset

To everyone at the Elephant House, Edinburgh, where this book was written, summer, 1996

And in happy memory of Children's Hour and the Scottish Home Service

CHAPTER ONE

Lady Maisie McNeil, not a day over 252 and as nimble as ever, slipped through the study window and seated herself before the gleaming computer. Exerting all her psychic strength, she switched it on, and then allowed her weightless fingers to play over the keyboard. The screen remained blank. Lady Maisie cursed, horribly but unheard. This was the third evening upon which she had battled against modern technology, and for the third time, she was defeated.

Defeat, however, was a word unknown to a McNeil. Lady Maisie, heroine of the famous Siege of Clachanfeckle, might find her powers fading, but her spirit remained undaunted.

She had not made the perilous journey forward to the twentieth century simply to be conquered by a mechanical beast. Come what may, she would have her revenge upon its master, the evil Robert Monteith—aye, upon him, the villainous, double-dealing, two-tongued rogue and all his family besides! The frippery, feather-pated sweetheart, her sulky black-browed daughter, and the impertinent, brown-haired miss. None would escape the wrath of Lady Maisie McNeil.

The ghost allowed herself to rise out of Robert's chair, borne aloft to the ceiling on a current of her own rage. As she rose, the draught from her invisible billowing skirt wafted aside the top sheet of Robert's carefully stacked notes, leaving a single trace of disorder in the otherwise tidy room.

*   *   *

'Rowan! Rowan!' Robert was approaching the ground floor of the house, calling loudly in his most serious, TV-documentary style voice.

Rowan sighed and slumped more deeply over the kitchen table. The only good thing about her name was that it was less awful than Blaeberry, which had been her mother's first choice.

However, even her mum had been forced to admit that her mousy-haired baby was unlikely to grow up into a darkly glamorous Blaeberry. Rowan had been next best—if you didn't mind sounding like a Flower Fairy.

It was also a name which sounded stupid when people shouted it, as Robert was doing now.

'Rowan!' He appeared in the doorway, still wearing his dark grey suit and striped shirt, but with his co-ordinating tie slightly loosened. What a prat, thought Rowan. He must be toasting on this hot summer's afternoon.

'Rowan, have you been nosing around in my study?'

Rowan raised her head very slightly, pushed back a straggle of hair and gave Robert the seriously dim look which she knew infuriated him. She held it for a slow count of ten.

'No, I haven't,' she said at last.

'Someone's been in there.'

'Wasn't me.'

'I can tell someone's been in.'

'Laid a trap, did you?'

Robert flushed. Seeing his handsome features go red, Rowan followed up the dim stare with an impudent grin and then, pulling her books towards her, buried herself in her homework.

Robert continued to hover in the doorway, so tall that his wavy dark hair almost touched the lintel. 'What nonsense, Rowan, of course I did no such thing. I can simply tell that someone's been in because the things on my desk are disarranged. I've told you before how vital it is that my notes are left in the correct order.'

'Why don't you ask Bryony?'

'She isn't here. Anyway, she wouldn't—!'

'How do you know? Ask her when she comes in.'

Rowan, although not looking up, had raised her voice.

'Ask who what, darling?' Petronella had come tripping down the hall in her little high-heeled sandals. She stood on tiptoe and kissed Robert, tilting her head back so that her tangle of streaked, strawberry blonde hair fell further down her back. 'Sweetheart, been home long?'

'Only just in.' Robert returned the embrace, but with an embarrassed glance in Rowan's direction.

Yeugh. Nothing was worse than having to watch this lovey-dovey rubbish. Rowan concentrated on her project on life in Edinburgh during the eighteenth century. If this had been 250 years ago, the elegant house in which she was sitting, old though it was, wouldn't have been built. She would actually have been in a field just outside the city, minding cows perhaps, or spreading washing to dry on the bushes.

'So ask who what?' repeated Petronella.

'One of the girls has been in my study, despite all I've said about no-one touching my desk.'

'Oh surely not!' Rowan's mum took a step backwards from her boyfriend. 'I just don't believe it. You must be mistaken.'

'I don't make that sort of mistake,' said Robert stiffly. 'I always leave my notes in a neat pile, but when I went in just now, the top pages were scattered all over the table.'

'A breeze then—'

'The window was shut.'

'Perhaps you slammed the door behind you when you left in the morning and the draught—'

'I. Did. Not. Slam. The. Door.'

Rowan observed with pleasure that Robert was going red again.

'Oh, hush, sweetheart, I'm sure you didn't.' Petronella waved her slim hands in Robert's direction, and then in Rowan's. 'Rowan, you're *sure* you didn't—?'

'No, I didn't,' said Rowan coldly.

Petronella stood helplessly between her two loved ones, still turning from one to the other. 'And it certainly wasn't *me*. I know better than to go into my big bear's very own private den.'

Oh cringe cringe cringe. Rowan almost groaned out loud. Did Mum have the least idea how daft she sounded? If this went on much longer, Rowan would have to take her homework upstairs, and that would be a pity because she knew that her presence in his kitchen annoyed Robert. That fact was worth a good deal of agony.

'Petronella, I didn't for a moment think—'

'You are such a fussboots about that study of yours! I blame your mother. Strict toilet training.'

'Nonsense.' Robert was melting under Petronella's blue eyes, just as Rowan knew he would. Mum, who had not forgotten her years as an actress, now completed her spell by throwing her arms around him.

'Anyway, there's no harm done. Probably just some nasty old sprite. Now why don't you go and get changed for supper, you must be boiling in that suit. I don't know why you bother to dress up—all your students wear jeans.'

'I just like to set an example.'

'Oh I know, if you wore jeans, everyone would think you were a student too.'

'Petronella, don't be ridiculous.' Robert gazed at her fondly.

'Not a bit. Now, are you going to

cook?' Petronella looked up at him hopefully.

'I could if you'd like me to.' Robert was beginning to smile again. 'I could make my tagliatelle.'

His tagliatelle indeed, thought Rowan. You'd think he was the only person in Scotland who could make Italian food.

'So are you going to ask Bryony about it when she comes in?'

The two adults stepped apart and looked down at Rowan. Petronella saw her adorable but mischievous younger daughter, whilst Robert saw the spoilt, sly brat whom he'd been obliged to take into his home because he loved Petronella so much.

'Now, darling, *don't* start all that again. It's past and forgotten about.'

'Well, you may have forgotten about it, Mum, but you're not the one who was accused of snooping.'

'You're exaggerating! Robert didn't *accuse* you—'

'Yes, he did.' Rowan looked very hard at Robert, something which she knew alarmed him. 'He said I'd been nosing around in his study.'

'Now, that's not true. I *asked* you—'

'Please, please!' Petronella covered her ears with her hands in a dramatic gesture. 'I've just spent the entire afternoon "Looking at Shakespeare" with my darling old ladies and I don't want any more excitement. *Both* say you're sorry.'

'Sorry,' barked Robert and, swinging round abruptly, he marched out of the room before Rowan could mutter her apology.

As Robert's footsteps died away on the stairs, the room settled back into being itself again. It was odd how, despite belonging to Robert, the kitchen looked so thoroughly Petronella's. The pretty old plates on the dresser, the frilly lace curtains, the pots of herbs along the window sill, they all formed, Rowan realized, a perfect background for her mother, much more so than had their old box of a kitchen in Yarrow Row.

Petronella sighed into the silence, and then, slipping off her pink silk jacket, sank down into the chair opposite Rowan's. Then she looked earnestly across at her.

'I know it's hard for you to get along with Robert,' she said, 'I do appreciate that. But you don't make any effort. You don't try to see his sweet side.'

Rowan, who had re-buried herself in the safety of her homework, snorted quietly.

'I know you find it hard to share your feelings about Robert, but it's better to talk about these things rather than keeping them bottled up.'

It was now Rowan's turn to have Petronella's huge eyes fixed upon her. Rowan gave in and said, 'There's not much point in *my* trying when *he* isn't. It's like, one law for adults and another for kids.'

'So your feeling is that Robert isn't working at your relationship?'

'Well, yes, if you want to put it like that.'

'But you need to make allowances for each other. Robert's never lived with young people before.'

'And I've never lived with my mother's boyfriend.' Rowan raised her head and looked sternly at her mother. Petronella, unlike Robert, did not blush. She leant forward across the waxed pine table and put her hand, laden with silver and amber and moonstone rings, over Rowan's.

'I know you miss Yarrow Row and all your old friends,' she said. 'That's only natural, you've lived there since you were born, but it needn't make you behave badly towards Robert. Can't you try to see him as being separate from anything you might feel about our moving house?'

Well, no, thought Rowan, but she knew from experience that saying so would simply involve her in an even longer and more embarrassing conversation.

'I'm sure we could all be happy together if you didn't challenge him all the time. Bryony doesn't.'

Bryony's solution to the Robert problem was just to pretend that he didn't exist.

'But he was the one who said I'd been in his study!'

'Robert is a very *private* person, it's

not easy for him suddenly sharing his home with three new people.'

Rowan wanted to say that it wasn't easy for *her,* suddenly sharing a home with Robert, but she didn't.

Petronella continued: 'You know, Robert would be really fond of you if you'd only give him a chance. He respects your intelligence.'

Rowan sniffed. 'Honestly, mum!'

'He does. I promise. Just don't be so hard on him.'

The trouble with Mum was that she was so pretty and appealing that you always ended up agreeing with her. There she sat, playing with some petals which had fallen onto the table from her cottagey flower arrangement, smiling straight into Rowan's eyes.

'OK,' said Rowan, smiling back. 'But you've got to admit, he does fuss about his precious study.'

Petronella threw up her hands with a rattle of bracelets and laughed. 'Yes, he does. He's an absolute baby about it. But it used to be his mother's room—perhaps that's got something to do with it. I mean, he never used to allow Alice to go in there either.'

Alice was Robert's wife.

'But what's he afraid of? None of us, not even Bryony, could understand what he's writing about.'

'I know. I'm always telling him he should write in simpler language. Bring economics to the common people.'

'Now what are you doing, talking about economics, Petronella?'

Robert had re-appeared in the kitchen doorway, now wearing dark blue linen slacks and a lighter blue Italian shirt, obviously a tagliatelle-cooking outfit. Rowan wondered what he'd wear for making hamburgers? Or Yorkshire pudding? Or, worst of all, haggis?

'And what's so funny, Rowan?'

'Nothing, Robert, really.'

'You were sniggering.'

'No, I wasn't.'

A look of deep disappointment was spreading over Petronella's face. 'Please. Good children. Don't quarrel. Please.'

Rowan got up, gathering her books into her arms. 'I think I'll just finish this upstairs.'

'You do that, darling. Make way for Masterchef.'

'Now you're doing it too, Petronella!'

Petronella's blue gaze was innocence itself. 'Doing what?'

'Sniggering.'

'You're too sensitive, Robert. No-one was laughing at you. Kiss and make up?'

Rowan hurried out of the room before she could witness any more revolting displays of affection. She supposed she was glad that her mother was happy, but why did she have to make such a song and dance about it?

CHAPTER TWO

Lady Maisie hovered a few feet above the half-landing, at the dark turn of the stair. To her mind, the writer's home was a miserable, poky place, far removed from the lofty splendours of Clachanfeckle Castle. Indeed, it seemed little more than a cottage, so small that the family could only fit inside because they were too poor to keep servants. The ghost curled her lovely lips in aristocratic scorn. Then, hearing the approach of the cross-patch little girl, she once more gathered up all her strength. If she could not influence the terrible machine, perhaps she could prevail upon the child to attack it for her?

Lady Maisie prepared to pounce.

Rowan came stamping up the stairs. Robert's house was actually a pretty Victorian villa, two storeyed, but with one room, the forbidden study, opening off the half-landing.

As she climbed towards it, Rowan

found herself mysteriously compelled to slow down. What was so special about Robert's room that he wouldn't allow anyone inside?

'Aye, my bairnie, just a peep, a peep won't do any harm, will it now?' Lady Maisie silently urged Rowan towards the door, chuckling to herself as she saw her hesitate. Her ghostly powers might no longer be great enough to influence machines, but she had not entirely lost her touch as far as mortals were concerned. And especially a young, headstrong mortal like this one.

Just look at her, ugly wee besom. Her hair wasn't bad, a curly light brown, not unlike Lady Maisie's own, but instead of being arranged in an elaborate cascade of ringlets, it barely reached her shoulders, where it was hauled back from her pale face with a scrap of gathered cloth. She had dark eyes, with long lashes, easily her best feature—but her garments! Certainly her skirt was cut from a good piece of Scottish plaid, but it was kilted up as short as a fisherlassie's, and her dark blue bodice had no shape to it

16

whatsoever. As for her poor feet, they were thrust into monstrous great bauchles. It was another sign of Robert Monteith's pitiful poverty that he could not clothe his lady's bairns half-decently.

Indeed, had Lady Maisie not been intent on her plan, she might have found it in her heart to pity the scowling little creature.

However, the heroine of Clachanfeckle was not one to be turned lightly aside from her goal. Just let her gain control of the child, and she would be on her way to victory.

The ghost beamed all the power at her command upon Rowan who, despite herself, found that she was reaching out for the doorknob. If Robert already thought she'd been poking around, she might as well make his suspicions come true. Down below she could hear his rich voice rolling out in his version of a Three Tenors aria, swiftly joined by Petronella's uncertain soprano. The coast was clear.

Without giving herself more time to think, Rowan opened the door and slipped inside. Then she took a deep breath and looked around. So what was so remarkable about the place? It was just a gloomy little room, the only window darkened by thick leaves which pressed up against the outside of the glass. The walls were lined with crammed bookshelves, whilst the centre of the room was taken up by Robert's sacred desk, upon which sat his computer and several books and folders, all of which were arranged in neat piles.

Rowan crept nearer the desk. There was nothing even remotely interesting here. Why had she given in to the strange urge to cross the threshold? All she could see were notes for Robert's latest dreary old book—books though, which were bought by enough people to make Robert quite wealthy. Since they'd come to live with him, Robert had given Petronella a car—no-one was allowed to touch his classic Volvo convertible—and insisted that she cut back on her teaching. He'd also bought Bryony her own clarsach, and he was paying Rowan's school fees.

However, there was no sign of his money in the study. Apart from the computer, the furnishings were old and battered, and unlike the rest of the house, the room was chilly, and even smelt a little musty. Rowan actually shivered. When they had moved in, almost six months ago, Petronella had swept through the house, making new curtains, painting, bringing out Robert's mother's pretty old china, but the study remained untouched. It reminded Rowan of how the whole place had once felt. Since his wife's mysterious departure, Robert had been living alone, and the house had had a bleak and sorrowful air. But Petronella had changed everything.

Except this room. It was the sort of room which made you want to tiptoe. Still not understanding why she'd been so eager to enter, Rowan turned back towards the door. And stopped dead. It was as though she'd walked into a column of icy cold air, and stepping back abruptly, she bumped into the desk. If it was always this cold, Robert must absolutely freeze as he sat, hour after hour, at his computer. Rowan looked at it more closely. The only new object in the room, it seemed to gleam enticingly at her. Robert, still singing merrily downstairs, would never know—Rowan jumped forward, almost as though someone had pushed her sharply between the shoulder blades, and reached for the keyboard. It was similar to the ones they had at school, so she had no problem in calling up Robert's menu. As the screen filled with entries, Rowan sighed so deeply that the sound seemed, ridiculously enough, to be echoed somewhere behind her. Honestly, each title was more boring than the next.

EC
Global
Chapter 07

Rowan closed the program and switched off the machine in disgust. It was just what she'd expected. Stupid old rubbish. She'd sneak out before Robert ever suspected that she'd touched his precious computer. However, yet again, it seemed strangely difficult actually to leave the room. Just as she touched the doorknob, a sudden draught, so cold and strong that it stirred the little hairs on the nape of her neck, made Rowan turn her head sharply. Could there be a crack in the wall behind the old cupboard? Was that why the room seemed so uncannily cold?

The space behind the door was taken up by a tall, old-fashioned bookcase with glass doors. The title of one of the volumes inside caught her eye: *Scottish Castles.* Next to it stood *A History of Scottish Costume.* She looked along the line of books. *Highland Dress. The Siege of Clachanfeckle*—and, wait a minute, *Edinburgh Past and Present*, just what she needed for her history project! Rowan grasped the little brass catch on the bookcase doors and tried to turn it. Nothing happened. Unbelievable! The books were locked in. None of the imprisoned volumes looked as though they were rare or expensive, just ordinary history books and guide books and books about famous people—the only thing they had in common was that they were all Scottish. Why on earth had Robert locked them up? And why did he have them in the first place? Not one of them had anything to do with cashflow or the European Community or common currency, the subjects which he usually found so enthralling.

Rowan suddenly realized that she was staring at her own frowning reflection in the glass, rather than at the rows of books beyond it. She seemed, for a moment, to have drifted off into a peculiar daydream, a dream in which she wasn't alone, but couldn't quite catch sight of her companion.

Ridiculous. That was all she needed, to be haunted by a creepy, half-remembering feeling, when all she wanted was for life to go back to being normal.

Rowan whirled round and dashed out of the study, not bothering about being quiet, and ran up the remaining stairs to her new bedroom. Of course she knew that things would never be really normal again, but it would help if life could settle down and at least begin to feel a bit ordinary. She supposed that Mum was right; she ought to try harder to get along with Robert. After all, she was getting used to her new school, even if she had no special friends there, and she no longer woke up every single morning wishing she were back in Yarrow Row. It was just Robert whom she couldn't stand. Why on earth had Mum decided to move in with him, and only two months after they'd met? After all, she'd had other boyfriends since Dad's departure, but none of them had changed her into this silly, housewife-person.

Rowan dropped her books onto the bed and sat down. She'd never put her nose into Robert's room again. It simply wasn't worth the risk of getting into more trouble. It didn't matter that he had the very books she needed for her project. It didn't matter that they were mysteriously locked up. She'd make herself forget the whole thing.

CHAPTER THREE

'Forget the whole thing indeed! Well, my fine young missy, we'll soon see about that.'

Lady Maisie had been in a frenzy ever since she'd failed to prevent the lassie from abandoning the machine. What had gone wrong? The words which she had read so eagerly on the glowing square were not those which she had watched Monteith tapping out, night after terrible night. Were those words still trapped somewhere inside the beast, and if so, how could she force the child to seek them out?

For a start, she could lead her back to the study by fanning her interest in the locked cupboard. So, sighing over the stupidity of humans, who couldn't pick up a ghost's thoughtwave as easily as she could pick up theirs, Lady Maisie followed Rowan down to supper.

For the next hour, the ghost sat comfortably on the top of the kitchen dresser, her slender feet tucked neatly in amongst old Mrs Monteith's plates. It grieved her that she was too weak to make her presence felt to the entire family, but she drew comfort from the way in which Rowan kept putting her hand to the back of her neck, as though a continual cold breeze blew upon her.

When the meal was over—and a sorrowful affair it had been, no great haunch of venison such as she had been wont to serve at Clachanfeckle, merely some cheesy slop and a mouthful of herbs—the fiendish Monteith made his way to his chamber, whilst the lassie with raven black hair was despatched to her music. One thing, at least, in the horrible latter-day world had remained the same. Lady Maisie, herself, had loved the outdoor life too much to make time for the harp, but it pleased her that the old tradition had not died out. She would have liked to follow the girl to the parlour to hear her play, but now that the wee miss was alone with her mother, it was time to strike again.

The ghost folded her hands in her

silken lap, and concentrated all her failing energy upon Rowan.

'Mum, what did Alice do?'

Until she heard herself saying them, Rowan had had no thought of speaking the words aloud. She was as surprised as Petronella, who turned to face her, a big salad bowl in her hands.

'Hush, Rowan! You know what she did, I told you. Robert doesn't like to talk about her, even although it all happened three years ago. She broke his heart by running away with that photographer.'

'No, Mum, I didn't mean that.' Now that she had started speaking, the words seemed to be forming themselves on her tongue, and then tumbling out, cold and solid as ice cubes. 'I mean, what did she do for a living? Was she a history teacher? For example.'

'Whatever gave you that idea? Alice, a history teacher!' Petronella stopped putting away dishes and looked at her daughter in astonishment.

Rowan, who was supposed to be helping, dropped some cutlery into the drawer with an unconcerned clatter. 'Oh, I don't know. Just the way the house was furnished when we first came. All these big gloomy pictures of Highland cattle and stuff.'

A sorrowful, rippling chord from Bryony's distant clarsach illustrated her words.

'No, these belonged to Robert's mother. He and Alice moved in here after she died, but I don't think Alice did much re-decorating.'

'Why not? It was terribly fusty.'

'She wasn't the sort of person who paid much attention to her surroundings. She was frightfully brainy, she did some sort of money thing, like Robert.'

'But if she was so like Robert, why did she run away?'

Although they were alone, Petronella glanced around and then lowered her voice. 'I don't believe she was *really* like Robert, not underneath. She was repressing her True Self.' Petronella enjoyed reading books on popular psychology, and it often showed in her speech. 'I think that when she met Nico, she realized that she was an explorer at heart, so when he asked her to climb the Andes with him, she just packed her rucksack and left!'

'Perhaps by the time she comes back, she'll have had enough adventure?' said Rowan hopefully.

'Well, she certainly won't be coming back here,' said Petronella firmly. She shut the drawer which Rowan had left open, and then, using the edge of her floral-print apron, whisked a few crumbs from the table top. Rowan, looking round the cosy, pretty room, knew what her mother meant. In a few months, Petronella had transformed Robert's life just as thoroughly as she had transformed a gloomy cavern into a bright kitchen. Even if Alice turned up, begging forgiveness for having deserted him, Robert would never want her back. Not now.

'So she wasn't specially interested in Scottish history or stuff like that?' Rowan returned to the subject she'd forbidden herself even to think about.

'Not as far as I know. Robert's

28

mother was fascinated by it, though. Apparently she was always going off on trips to castles and what not. And she had dozens of those soppy historical novels by Marjorie Gloaming. I put them in the attic, along with all that stuff which Alice left. Robert was actually a bit cross, but honestly, I couldn't have them cluttering up the drawing room.'

'But weren't there any sort of serious books? I mean, you'd think that if she were interested enough to go to castles and stuff, she'd have at least *some* history books.'

Petronella stopped in the middle of hanging up her apron. 'Funny that. I've never thought about it. I suppose they'd be in Robert's study. If there are any.'

'I just thought there might be something useful—you know, for my project.'

'*What* a good idea! You are *such* a clever pet. I'll run up and ask him.'

'But he's working!'

'I'll just put my head round the door.' And Petronella dashed away, her long swirly skirt whisking round the door after her. That was typical of Mum, thought Rowan. When she got an idea, she forgot about being silly, and became brisk and practical. But it did look as though the Mystery of the Locked Bookcase wasn't really a mystery at all. All the Scottish books must have belonged to Robert's mother, and Robert simply kept them locked up because he never bothered to look at them. Rowan felt quite disappointed. She would have enjoyed seeing Robert as the keeper of a dark secret. She could have unmasked him, and then Petronella would have been sorry that she'd ever made her daughters leave home. And in fact, as their old house was only rented out, they could probably—

'He hasn't got any.'

'What?' Rowan came back to earth to see Petronella standing in the doorway.

'He says he gave all his mother's books to a friend of hers. Apart from those rubbishy things I put in the attic.'

'Oh.' Rowan knew her mouth must

be hanging open, but she didn't seem able to close it.

'Sorry about that, darling. But there's always the library. Is there something special you wanted? I could go along with you and help you find it.' Petronella clasped her hands together prettily. Since she'd dragged Rowan and Bryony away from their old life, she was constantly trying to make it up to them.

'No. Nothing special.' As usual, Rowan took a horrible, guilty pleasure in rejecting mum's desire to be extra nice to her.

'Oh, very well. You know you've only got to ask.' And Petronella left the kitchen quickly, not looking at Rowan.

Rowan knew she'd hurt her mother, but she didn't care. No-one had asked her if she'd wanted to leave Yarrow Row, where she knew everybody, and where she could go round to Natalie's or Colette's every day after school. She went over to the window and stared out into the sunlit garden. No Scottish history books! But Robert had an entire *cupboard* full of books all about

Scotland! Why was he lying about them? Didn't he want anyone to touch these precious relics of his mother? One mystery had simply been replaced by another.

Rowan sank down into the nearest chair. Despite the warm scented air coming through the open window, she felt terribly cold. It seemed that bland, ordinary Robert was turning into a figure of mystery after all. What did she really know about him, apart from the fact that her mother was making a fool of herself over him?

Rowan pulled Mum's shopping pad towards her, and began making a list of her own:

1) Robert writes very dull books
2) He has a lot of money
3) He has somehow cast a spell over Mum
4) He doesn't have any family
5) His wife disappeared three years ago to climb the Andes, and has never been heard from since
6) He has just lied about the contents of his locked cupboard

Rowan studied her list for a moment, and then, very quickly, scribbled a second one.

1) Perhaps Alice never went to South America
2) Perhaps she had a lot of money
3) Perhaps Robert *murdered* Alice and has hidden her body in his study.

That would explain both why he was so well-off and why he didn't want anyone poking around in his room! It was nothing to do with the books. He was afraid that poor Alice's skeleton might somehow be discovered. Because she must be a skeleton by now. Perhaps he hadn't meant actually to kill her— they could've been having a row, and he'd pushed her, and she'd fallen and hit her head against that big cupboard . . .

But in that case, how could he bear to go on working in the very room where his young wife had died? No, it was more likely that he'd murdered her in cold blood and then bricked up her body in the wall behind the bookcase.

With a terrible secret like that concealed in his room, no wonder he allowed no-one to enter!

CHAPTER FOUR

Rowan, frozen with horror, was unaware of the small commotion immediately under the ceiling.

Lady Maisie was stamping silently upon the top shelf of the dresser. What was the daft wee blether on about? The ghost had already assumed that Monteith's wife was dead, and whether or not her body was hidden behind the study wall was no concern of hers. What the silly girl was meant to do was to take revenge upon Monteith for the terrible wrong which he had done to her, Lady Maisie, and not to some mere wife. In Lady Maisie's time it was nothing out of the ordinary for an inconvenient wife to be quietly murdered, so why make such a fuss about it? Thank goodness she had perished bravely before she had been obliged to marry.

The girl had now got up and was pacing round the table, clutching her arms about herself as though she were cold. Once again, Lady Maisie cursed her own weakness. Was this the most she could do, make a mortal shiver? She remembered the happy days after her death when her powers had been so great that she had driven generations of owners out of Clachanfeckle Castle. But alas, over the years her strength had faded, and she had actually been unable to prevent the present heir from turning her beloved home into a vulgar tavern. And now this, the final and most terrible indignity! She was too frail to protect her good name. Monteith toyed with it as he pleased and she was powerless to prevent him.

The ghost actually shed tears of mingled fury and grief, which appeared as drops of burning dew upon Petronella's flower arrangement.

And all the while, there stood the lassie, shaking in her horrible great laced shoes because she thought she had found out Monteith's secret. Aye, little did she know that Monteith's crime was more gruesome than any mere murder!

For a moment, the ghost despaired. But it was not in Lady Maisie's valorous nature to despair for long, so after wringing her hands a few times, and pacing once or twice along the shelf, she floated downwards a few feet, to hover behind Rowan.

Rowan shivered, shook herself, and going over to the window, closed it. Why did she feel so cold when it wasn't yet night? The evening sun still slanted in between the trees, lying in warm pools upon the beds of foxgloves and sweet william and old, tangled roses. Perhaps she was ill? But she didn't feel ill. Just cold. She would make herself a cup of tea. But even as she turned to pick up the kettle, something urged her out of the kitchen, down the hallway, and up the stairs. She would go and huddle under her duvet until she felt warmer. And this time there would be no temptation to creep into Robert's study as she passed, because he would be in there, hard at work.

However, just as she reached the half-landing, Rowan heard Robert's voice from the open door of the drawing room. He must have gone down to listen to Bryony play. Robert, who loved music, took a great interest in her progress, despite the fact that Bryony did her best to pretend that he wasn't there.

'I loved that piece you played just now,' he was saying. 'Lady Nairn's Fancy, wasn't it?'

Silence.

'I thought I recognized it.'

'I've never heard of a tune called Lady Nairn's Fancy. *That* was the Rakes of Mallow.'

He'd give up in a moment. He wasn't as afraid of Bryony as he was of Rowan, so he tried harder to get to know her. Rowan knew, however, that it was a doomed attempt. If Bryony decided she didn't like a person, that was it. Sometimes Rowan felt almost sorry for Robert as he plunged on and on, trying to be interesting to a teenager, whilst Bryony simply looked at him blankly through her little designer glasses.

And there he was, still trying. 'I've really got a lot to learn,' he was now saying, with a hearty, patronizing laugh.

Rowan decided she could risk one swift look round the study door before he returned upstairs. She pushed it open, and, trembling slightly, peered round the edge.

Now, if she were to hide a body in the tiny room, where would she begin?

Rowan curled herself right round the door so that she could see the cupboard. Then she stopped dead, locked with astonishment into a spiral.

The glass doors had been lined with brown paper so that it was impossible to see the books inside.

'OK, got to get back to work. I must say I think it's wonderful to have real music in the house again. My mother used to play the piano all the time—it's something I've missed.'

Then the drawing room door closed, and Robert could be heard walking down the hall, humming melodiously.

Rowan instinctively unknotted herself, bounded backwards onto the landing, pulled the door shut, and darted upstairs to her own room. There she flung herself onto the bed and clutched Mr Bear, the friend whose company she hadn't quite outgrown.

Up until that moment, the mystery had been pleasantly scary. Rowan hadn't truly believed that Robert had murdered Alice and then stuffed her body behind the cupboard, but *pretending* that she believed it had given her another reason for hating him. But now that she had a genuine reason for being suspicious, it was alarming rather than exciting.

First he had lied about having the books, and then he had actually hidden them. Rowan propped herself up against the pillows, hugging Mr Bear so tightly that her shoulders hurt. For once, her new room with its matching flowery wallpaper and frilled curtains failed to soothe her. She used to think that if only she could have a room of her own rather than being squashed into an attic with Bryony, she'd be completely happy. Now that she realized how wrong she had been, all she wanted was to undo the wish and find herself back in Yarrow Row. She'd

40

even be prepared to share with Bryony again.

At the thought of her elder sister, Rowan slithered off the bed, tucked Mr Bear under the duvet and padded across the thick green carpet to the door. Through the wall she could hear the surging wail of Bryony's CD player, so she'd obviously finished practising and returned upstairs. Bryony always kept her music separate, playing the gentle clarsach downstairs, and listening to her favourite miserable, bad-tempered singers in her own room. When Rowan opened the door, the noise was overwhelming. Bryony was lying on her bed, in a sort of book-lined nest, listening to some woman yowling about her unhappy life to a spiky piano accompaniment. At Rowan's approach, Bryony raised her tangled black head, and glared.

Bryony had the same curly mouse hair as Petronella and Rowan, but just as her mother's had grown blonder, Bryony's had turned a dramatic, overnight black shortly after their arrival in Dryburgh Place.

'What do you want?' she said.

'Oh, mm, nothing. What are you doing?'

'Essay.'

Bryony, despite her dyed hair, ferocious eyeliner and nose ring, always got top marks. She had refused to join Rowan at nearby St Agnes's, but took a bus every day back to her old high school. Thus, unlike Rowan, she didn't have to wear a uniform of tartan skirt and blue T-shirt, and at the moment was clad in a small black top, miniskirt and black tights.

'Was that you speaking to Robert downstairs?'

'The wuss.'

Rowan sat down on Bryony's bed. Bryony hadn't allowed Petronella to redecorate, so her room was unchanged since Robert's mother's time, with curly brown matching furniture, and crinkly wallpaper patterned with orange and brown autumn leaves. Bryony claimed to be above her surroundings, like the mysterious Alice. She also claimed that as she'd be leaving the minute she got her Highers, it wasn't worthwhile painting her room. She hadn't even put up her posters from Yarrow Row, which remained stacked in a corner.

'Bryony?'

'Working.' Robert wasn't the only person to whom Bryony didn't talk.

'Have you ever been in Robert's study?'

'Course not.'

'But haven't you ever wondered what it was like inside?'

'No.'

'But aren't you curious about it? I mean, he makes such a fuss about our not going in.'

'Well, I don't like people coming into my room either.' Bryony looked meaningfully at Rowan through her glasses. As she had chosen these before her transformation, the dainty speckled frames looked odd above her nose ring.

'But you don't go on about it like he does.'

'If I had a computer like his, I might.'

'He said he'd buy you a computer. Well, us.'

'I don't want his—computer,' said

Bryony, using words which were forbidden at Rowan's polite new school. 'You and Mum may have sold out to him, but that doesn't mean I have to.'

'But you let him buy you a clarsach.'

'That was different.'

'So how's it different?'

'I needed my own clarsach. I couldn't go on borrowing one.'

Bryony had been playing the small Scottish harp since primary school. Rowan kept expecting her to give it up, now that she wore make-up and stayed out late, but she actually played more than ever, as though she found comfort in the soft, familiar tones. It was also her last link with their musician father, whom Bryony remembered so much better than Rowan. Rowan had been only three when he finally failed to return from a series of gigs in Germany.

'But we need our own computer too.'

'Well, you just suck up to Robert for a couple of days and he'll buy you one. He's falling over himself to give us stuff.' And Bryony began building her books into a wall between her sister and herself.

Rowan, seeing this, said desperately, 'But, Bry, wouldn't you *like* to see inside his study? We could go in sometime when he's at the university, just see what he's up to.'

'But we *know* what he's up to. Writing.'

'That's what he says.'

'It's not just what he says, he's got all the books to prove it.'

'But don't you think there's something mysterious about him? And Alice—the way she just disappeared?' Rowan leant hopefully towards her sister across the book barricade.

'No.'

'But Bryony—'

'I said "No".' Bryony pushed aside her fringe and looked properly at Rowan. 'Look, Rowan, just go away. I don't give a scooby about Robert or his study, and as for Alice, I'm only surprised she didn't shove off sooner. And turn the sound up as you go, could you?'

The mournful vocalist was already,

in Rowan's opinion, singing quite loudly enough, but she turned the volume up still further, and retreated to her own room.

Obviously, Bryony was going to be no help. If she wanted to find out Robert's secret, she would have to do it alone.

CHAPTER FIVE

'Aha, no, my lassie, you will not fight alone!'

Lady Maisie was seated in Rowan's rocking chair, watching her incompetent assistant with scorn. Too insubstantial actually to rock, the ghost merely caused the chair to quiver slightly, and Rowan, wrapped in her own thoughts, did not notice. Lady Maisie, exasperated, threw herself against the back of the chair. The quivering increased slightly, but that was all. For the first time in her other-worldly existence, Lady Maisie felt a tremor of fear.

'Blethers and havers!' she exclaimed in silence. 'Alive or dead, I, Lady Maisie McNeil of Clachanfeckle, have never been afraid. And I have no intention whatever of starting now!'

But for all her brave words, she trembled. She knew that a ghost's power fades with each passing year and as, in her case, the 252nd anniversary of her death was fast approaching, her haunting days were numbered. This she could have accepted had it not been for the terrible discovery she had so recently made, a discovery which had left her shaking with fury—and with this first glimmer of fear.

There she had been, those few short nights ago, drifting happily down Dryburgh Place through the warm June dusk, her head full of the sweet old Scottish tunes which the elderly lady who had once lived there used to play. Many a time the ghost had sat, unseen, on top of the piano, tapping her foot, and remembering the times when she'd danced until dawn to that very music.

Then, alas, the old lady's place had been taken by Alice, her son's brash young wife, who had slammed down the piano lid and shoved the instrument into a corner. In revenge at losing her music, Lady Maisie had summoned her failing powers to play a few tricks upon the woman, curdling the milk, or edging a dish from shelf to floor. Until the humiliating evening

48

when the woman, entering the kitchen in time to see a plate skim across the room, had seized a fistful of salt and flung it towards the corner where Lady Maisie lurked. The tiny, stinging grains had gone clean through the ghost's pretty face, and skirling with wrath, she had retreated from the house.

If there is one thing a ghost cannot abide, it is the magical and cleansing power of salt.

However, that had been over three years ago. Time now, perhaps, for another cantrip? Humming mischievously, Lady Maisie had hovered above the shadowy garden, watching the dark house. Only one window was lit, that of the small room where the old mistress had sometimes sat to write or sew. Swooping to the sill and peering in, the ghost had seen Robert, the good-for-nothing son, sitting before a mysterious machine, a sleek contraption whose surfaces reflected light like the skirt of her favourite silk gown.

The ghost, curiosity-stricken, had slithered through the glass and cautiously circled man and machine.

At first, she could hardly believe her eyes. As he touched the keys, letters appeared on the glowing, indeed ghostly, screen, forming neatly printed words. What magical device was this? Despite herself, the ghost was impressed. This was so much swifter than the blotchy quill pen of her own days. Indeed, had she had this machine at her command, she would have written her own story, and her fame would have spread, not just to Edinburgh, but to foreign lands beyond.

But alas, no handier with the pen than she had been with the clarsach, Lady Maisie had left no word behind her, and now, too late, she regretted the hours she had spent in riding and dancing, and aye, fighting.

She regretted them because now, to her horror and disbelief, it was her own name which she saw form under Robert's fingers.

The words leapt onto the screen:

'Help! Help! Save me!' The lovely Maisie McNeil fled across the heather,

the red-coated English soldiers gaining upon her as her strength failed.

'Never fear, Lady Maisie, I am here!' It was young Lord Ronald on his gallant charger, drawn sword in hand. 'I will save you!'

Lady Maisie sobbed with relief as Lord Ronald swept her up before him onto the saddle. 'We'll soon outrun these English rogues,' he cried valiantly.

The ghost could bear to read no more. Shrieking with rage, she had hurled herself at Robert, tugging his hair with icy fingers.

'You dare write that yon miserable milksop, Lord Ronald, rescued *me*, Lady Maisie McNeil of Clachanfeckle! Never, never, never! It was I who defended my castle against the redcoats whilst he fled across Rannoch! Lying beast! Take back your evil words!'

Robert, totally unconcerned, had continued to type.

It was then that Lady Maisie had realized that the unthinkable had finally happened.

She could no longer influence the living world.

And so, for three dreadful nights, Lady Maisie had returned to haunt Robert's study. And always with the same result. Robert remained unaware of her presence. Certainly he might rub his cold hands together or peer suspiciously into the corners of the room, but then he'd cease fidgeting, and return to his fiendish work, happy as before.

'As though I would ever flee from the redcoats!' the ghost had moaned, night after night. 'It was Ronald who fled, whilst I stayed to fight!'

Lady Maisie might be a ghost, but she was no fool. Once she had realized what was happening, she had set herself to puzzling out just why Monteith was slandering her.

Could her teasing have driven his salt-flinging wife away, and this was his revenge? No, if the woman was no longer about, she had more likely died of a fever, or in childbed, as wives so frequently did in Lady Maisie's day. Or, indeed, Monteith himself might have murdered her, as the lassie suspected. No black deed was beyond him.

Or perhaps Monteith's clan held some deep grudge against hers?

Or was he one of those cowardly historians who sit safe in their studies and write about battles, once those who fought them are all dead and can do nothing to defend their honour?

Aye, that seemed the most likely. Lady Maisie looked with scorn at Robert's ironed shirt, and clean hands. The man had never wielded a broadsword in his life. He must be writing some fusty little history book about the rebellion in which she had played so brave a part, but he was such a dolt that he had twisted the entire episode, making out that the wretched Ronald was a hero!

And she had no way of protecting her good name.

Robert paid her little heed. She was too weak and too ignorant to affect the computer. She had fluttered around Petronella and Bryony, but in vain. The mother was too much in love to attend to a ghost, and the daughter had no room in her painted head for the supernatural. Lady Maisie's spirits had lifted when she first heard the sweet strains of the clarsach—the tune was one which Monteith's mother had played, and to which she had often danced—and she had floated to the parlour in an excited rush of cold air. But alas! Feeling the draught, the haughty miss had simply put on a woollen jerkin and continued to play.

That had left Rowan.

And now, at last, the ghost was having some success. The child was certainly aware of her presence, even if she was unsure as to what, exactly, was ruffling the edges of her consciousness. And she was already becoming suspicious of Robert. And Robert, himself, had played into her ghostly hand by hiding his books. Obviously the rogue had the grace to be ashamed of writing lies, and was attempting to hide his deceit from his sweetheart and her children, but she would unmask him.

With the help of the innocent little girl.

And Lady Maisie, rocking very

slightly, looked at Rowan, who lay curled up on the bed, cuddling her babyish animal doll—the ghost's favourite toy had been her little wooden sword—and she laughed.

CHAPTER SIX

'I had the most awful dream last night.'

'Oh, sweetheart, was it so very bad?'

'I've just said so, haven't I?'

'Well, darling, you needn't be cross. I was just sympathizing.'

Rowan knew she should have realized that this was a bad moment to attract her mother's attention. This was Petronella's morning for taking a drama workshop for senior citizens and she was fussing around the kitchen stuffing scripts and paper and pens into her bag, pausing only to fuel herself with another sip of black coffee. Robert, who had been working late, was still asleep, and Bryony had already departed for her distant high school.

'So what sort of awful was it?' Petronella, obviously deciding that her uprooted daughter's problems were more important than being on time for her class, sat down properly. Her concerned expression looked odd beneath her be-ribboned ponytail, but Rowan felt no desire to giggle. She laid down her toast and said: 'It was something about a staircase. I had to catch up with someone. I climbed as fast as I could, but she was always just ahead of me.'

'She?'

Rowan, who had been making patterns with the crumbs on her plate, looked up, disconcerted.

'Yes. I hadn't thought about it until I said it. She. And there was a lot of smoke and we were both being chased.'

'But that sort of dream's quite common. I mean, I have dreams in which I'm being chased.' Petronella flicked her tail of highlighted hair, and Rowan had the distinct feeling that the people who chased her mother were completely different from her terrifying, unseen pursuers.

'But it was scary.' It had been a lot worse than scary, but somehow Rowan didn't know how to describe the choking feeling which still haunted her.

'Well, if you go on having these dreams, perhaps you'd like to talk to

Mollie about them?' Mollie, one of Petronella's oldest friends, was a therapist who specialized in treating disturbed children. Ever since Mum had whisked Rowan away from her old life in Yarrow Row, she had been suggesting that she talk to Mollie.

'I don't think they're that bad,' said Rowan hastily. She was determined not to be put in a box marked 'disturbed'. 'I don't think I need to bother Mollie, thank you.'

'Well, as you like, darling. It seems that everything I suggest is wrong. Going to the library together. Speaking to Mollie.' And Petronella jumped up and flew back into her lovable, scatty mother routine. 'You have got everything? Lunch money? More to the point, have *I* got lunch money? Yes. No. Well, bank card, that'll do, provided I remember to go to the bank.'

In the old days, they'd all had economy-cheddar sandwiches for lunch, which Petronella had got up early to make for them. Bryony still made herself this type of sandwich, always choosing the cheapest of the four or five cheeses to be found in Robert's fridge, but Rowan had to admit that she enjoyed going to the deli every lunchtime and buying a big Italian roll stuffed with smoked turkey or ham and salad.

She felt a twinge of guilt as she checked her purse, finding several pound coins and a couple of fifty pences. If she really disliked Robert so much, the least she could do was to behave like Bryony and stop taking his money.

'Off in a dream as usual. I said, do you need lunch money?'

'No, not today.'

'Hurry up then, don't you be late even if I am. I wonder if Robert's awake? Should I take him up some coffee before I dash off?'

Rowan, putting on her blazer and shouldering her bag, already knew the answer. Why did Mum even bother to ask? She'd make herself even later by setting Robert a dainty little tray with his favourite big French cup and saucer, a tiny jug of cream, and a cafetière of his special breakfast blend which no-one else was allowed to drink.

'See you, Mum.' Rowan slammed out the back door into the still-dewy garden.

'Don't forget what I said about Mollie!' Petronella called after her.

Rowan, pushing aside the tendrils of honeysuckle which threatened to knot the gate shut for ever, like the entrance to the Sleeping Beauty's castle, counted up the things which she couldn't forget, no matter how hard she tried.

The new clothes and pocket money which Petronella gave her, but which really came from Robert. The locked cupboard in his study. The mysterious disappearance of his wife. And the dream.

Now that she was hurrying along the narrow lane, overhung with ivy and rambling roses, which ran between the back gardens of Dryburgh Place and neighbouring Jedburgh Terrace, the memory should have faded, blown away by the sweet smelling morning air. Yet although she was walking along the narrow strip of sunshine which warmed one side of the lane, Rowan couldn't shake off a persistent chill.

And the very odd feeling that someone was running lightly ahead of her, too swiftly to appear in view.

Alice?

CHAPTER SEVEN

Rowan thrust herself free of the duvet and scrabbled for the switch to her bedside light. She was choking and gasping so badly that for a terrible moment she thought the house was on fire, but as her finger found the switch and she was contained in the calm pool of light, she realized that it was only the dream, returned, for the second night running, to haunt her.

Still struggling for breath, Rowan told herself firmly not to be a baby. Afraid of the dark indeed, at her age. And terrified of dreams! She'd get up right now and check for smoke, just to prove that it was a dream and that she wasn't scared. Holding Mr Bear firmly under her arm, Rowan jumped out of bed, tiptoed to the door, and looked out cautiously. The upper landing was lit brightly by the full moon which shone through the gracefully arched window. No smoke, no noise, everything in order.

To make completely sure that all was well, Rowan padded to the top of the staircase.

There was a line of light under the study door. She knew, from Petronella's prettily aggrieved comments, that Robert often worked late, so this was nothing unusual. Rowan turned, intending to go thankfully back to bed, but almost as though a firm, cold hand were pushing her in the small of the back, she found herself descending, step by step, towards the tiny beam of light. By the time she reached the half-landing, the icy patch at the centre of her body had spread to her limbs and she was shaking all over. Yet she couldn't stop herself from creeping ever nearer the forbidden door.

Then, almost on the threshold, Rowan heard steps approaching from the other side of the door. Without knowing how she did it, Rowan leapt down the remaining stairs, her feet somehow finding the treads in the dark, and crouched in the alcove behind the newel post.

Almost before she'd reached her

hiding place, Robert appeared above her, outlined by the light from the now open door. He ran lightly down the stairs, passing Rowan, hunched in the shadows, and disappeared into the kitchen. Immediately, the kitchen light flipped on, and he could be heard moving dishes with a soft clatter.

Rowan held Mr Bear tightly against her wildly beating heart. Robert was probably making himself some of the strong coffee he drank while he worked, so that gave her at least five minutes in which to get safely back upstairs. And anyway, why shouldn't she be wandering around the house? Robert kept telling her it was her home now, didn't he?

Taking deep, even breaths, Rowan began to climb the staircase, placing her bare feet softly in the centre of each carpeted step. Robert had left his door open, so this time she could at least see where she was going. But inevitably, as she reached the spot where the light from the study spread over the half-landing, Rowan turned sharply, like a soldier on parade, and entered the forbidden room.

Robert had obviously been hard at work. Several books lay open round the computer, which was still switched on, and others were piled on the floor. Rowan glanced swiftly around. The locked bookcase stood open, one papered door angled into the room, and behind it, the books lolled untidily on the shelves, collapsing over gaps in their ranks.

Knowing what she would find, Rowan walked right into Robert's room and looked down at his desk. Yes, it was his mother's books which lay open there, and his own economic textbooks which had been banished to the floor.

Somehow, Rowan wasn't in the least surprised. All the books were open at illustrations of women in old-fashioned costume. One, a drawing of a woman gracefully wrapped in a plaid shawl, was entitled 'A Townslady, 1746'. Another was a portrait of a pretty young lady in a low-necked tartan gown, a lace frill falling away from her slender hand, and in that hand, which she held against her bosom, just as Rowan was holding Mr Bear, was a perfect white rose. Rowan knew that the rose meant that 'Lady Maisie McNeil of Clachanfeckle, by an unknown artist' was a follower of the romantic, doomed Prince Charles Edward Stuart.

And what a lovely face the long-dead Maisie had! Completely forgetting that the book's owner might appear at any moment, Rowan actually picked it up in order to look more closely. Lady Maisie seemed to smile at her with an air of irresistible mischief and charm, eyebrows arched, and the corners of her mouth just twitching up. You could imagine that the instant the artist laid down his brush, she'd whirl away to a ball, or out to the stables. Even in a picture, this Lady Maisie looked too full of life to keep still.

Rowan found herself sighing deeply. How sad that this pretty creature, who, according to the book, had perished during an attack on Clachanfeckle Castle by the English army, should be painted with a smile on her face, unaware of her approaching fate.

Her sigh was so heartfelt and so deep, that it seemed to echo around the room, almost as though someone else were sighing beside her. Poor Lady Maisie!

'Rowan!'

Rowan leapt a good two inches, dropping both the book and Mr Bear.

Robert was standing in the doorway. In his hands, which were shaking almost as much as hers, he held a tray of rattling coffee pot, cream jug, and mug.

'Rowan!' Despite his fury and surprise, he was attempting to keep his voice down. 'What the *hell* are you doing here?'

CHAPTER EIGHT

Rowan felt at a terrible disadvantage. Usually she could stare Robert down, or play upon his guilt at having disturbed her family, but now she was so obviously in the wrong that she could feel herself curling up in embarrassment. When she looked down, she could actually see her bare toes trying to bury themselves in the carpet.

'Hello, Robert,' she said, making a feeble attempt at her exasperating grin. 'I was just passing.'

She knew she must look pretty silly, wearing her favourite nightshirt with the numbered sheep on it, and with Mr Bear sprawled at her feet. She bent down to pick up her friend, and retrieved Robert's book at the same time.

'This is a lovely book,' she said. 'It doesn't seem to have much to do with economics though.'

'It certainly does,' snapped Robert.

'The amount of money which people have to spend on clothes is an excellent indication of a country's economic health.'

Like Rowan, he seemed determined to recover from his surprise. He put his tray down on the desk, shut all the open books, added the one Rowan held to the pile, and closed down the computer. Before the screen went blank, Rowan had time to glimpse the words *holding up her silken skirt in one hand, she approached the gallant chieftain.*

'I'm currently writing an account of economic policies during the reign of King George II and how these were affected by the necessity of suppressing the Scottish rebellion of 1745,' said Robert.

'You're what?' Rowan was still staring at the empty screen. Silken skirt? Gallant chieftain?

'They don't teach you anything in school these days.' Robert strode past her to the bookcase, closed the papered doors, locked them, and put the key into the pocket of his linen slacks. 'In 1745 several of the Scottish clans supported the claim of Prince Charles Edward Stuart to the throne, against that of King George, an ancestor of our present Queen. George's English army, the redcoats, quashed the rebellion, Prince Charles fled, and the Highlands of Scotland became occupied territory.'

Despite the unpleasantness of her situation, Rowan couldn't help being interested. 'I did know that,' she said. 'I'm actually doing a project on life in Edinburgh during the 18th century.'

'I can guess what that's going to be like,' said Robert dismissively. 'Women wearing hooped petticoats, and emptying their chamber pots in the street. Now go to bed and don't let me catch you snooping around my room again.'

'I wasn't *snooping*,' said Rowan loftily. 'I was doing *research*.'

And in as much as she could sweep, in her bare feet and carrying a toy animal, she swept past Robert and up the stairs.

After the girl's departure, Robert's

room seemed inexplicably colder, but he poured himself some hot coffee and got back to work.

Holding up her silken skirt with one hand, she approached the gallant chieftain.

'Will you dine with us the night?' she said, a blush upon her lovely face.

But Robert couldn't concentrate. What had the wretched brat meant by 'doing research'? Research for her ridiculous school project, he supposed. She must have seen the books, got Petronella to enquire about them, and now she actually had the nerve to come poking around his room! However, he'd put her off the scent pretty cleverly with his story about a history book. She'd never suspect the truth.

Robert forced himself to relax. Then he spread out his fingers, a master of the silent keyboard.

Lord Ronald bent over the pretty hand. 'You do me too much honour,' he said.

'On the contrary, sir, no honour is too great for the man who saved me from the redcoats.'

Soon Robert was smiling contentedly, absorbed in his secret world.

*   *   *

Rowan was sitting up in bed, still shivering from the shock of the encounter with Robert.

He was lying. A book about economics, no matter how historical, would hardly be describing gallant chieftains and girls in silken dresses. And why was Robert bothering to lie? Who cared what boring old book he was writing next? And he'd been so angry when he found her in his room! There must be something worse than a few mouldy old books hidden there.

When she thought what the worst thing might be, she found herself growing colder and colder.

Once again, she failed to notice the quivering rocking chair.

Lady Maisie was flinging herself backwards and forwards in a frenzy. Of all the numbskulls she'd ever dealt with, including the unbelievably stupid Lord Ronald, this lassie was the worst.

72

She had led her straight to Monteith's chamber, she had laid out the evidence of his treachery before her, yet the bairn was still blethering away to herself about economics, whatever they were, and books and secrets and mysteries. The so-called mystery was as plain as a pikestaff, but even when shown Lady Maisie's portrait, all the girl could do was sit there, frightening herself with visions of skeletons.

At the thought of her portrait, however, Lady Maisie softened slightly, and rocked more slowly and dreamily. Aye, she had been beautiful, and sprightly with it. The ghost stretched out her dainty foot, shod in a soft leather shoe laced with scarlet ribbons. If only she could make Monteith see her, she could surely charm him into giving up his book, just as she had charmed her father into letting her neglect her lessons, and Lord Ronald into giving her his favourite horse . . . For a moment, the ghost was lost in happy memories. Then, as Rowan doused the magic candle which lit the room so brightly without a single flicker, Lady Maisie was returned briskly to the present.

Did the lassie think she would be allowed to sleep peacefully when she had just failed so miserably in her appointed task?

Lady Maisie, smiling grimly, used her favourite new phrase.

'No chance, lassie, no chance.'

CHAPTER NINE

'Are you feeling all right, Rowan darling?' Petronella paused in her flutter around the breakfast table.

'Why shouldn't I be?'

'You've got enormous dark circles under your eyes.'

Obviously Robert had kept their midnight meeting secret. He must feel as guilty as she did.

'I'm OK.'

'Was it that dream again?'

'What dream?' Bryony, in witchlike black from beret to trainers, paused in the doorway, her bag over her shoulder.

'Nothing.'

'Rowan had this dream in which she was chasing someone up a staircase, and someone else was chasing her and—'

'Oh!'

'Something wrong with you too, lovey?'

A startled look had appeared on

Bryony's face. 'Nothing. 'Bye.' And she hurried out, her normal expression of total blankness carefully restored.

'Oh, you girls are complete mysteries to me!' Petronella cried, her hands rising and falling elegantly through the air.

Lady Maisie, from her seat on top of the dresser, admired the woman's grace. She must dance very prettily. It was only a shame that she was so hopelessly silly. And look how badly she had brought up her daughters! She allowed her children to address her with a complete lack of respect. If she, Lady Maisie, had spoken so rudely to her elders when she was a bairn, she would have been whipped and sent to the nursery.

But the child was speaking again. Lady Maisie was actually a little sorry to see how worn, and indeed, haunted, she looked this morning, but the ghost hardened her heart. Pity had no part in her plan. Until the lassie understood her bidding and destroyed the words, she must suffer.

'Mum, what's Robert's latest book

about?'

'Oh, the usual thing—money, cash flow, inflation—you know I don't really understand what he does.' Petronella made a silly-little-me face.

'But is it a book on *modern* economics?'

'I don't know really. I suppose so.'

Rowan felt like shaking her mother. She knew that Petronella wasn't nearly as frivolous as she liked to appear, but since they'd moved in with Robert, the sensible, wage-earning mother had slipped further and further out of sight.

'But he must have mentioned it.'

'It's just that if he does talk about it, I don't actually listen because I don't understand. But I appreciate your taking an interest. Why don't you ask him yourself?'

Because I don't think he'd tell me the truth, thought Rowan.

'You're still looking odd, darling. Do you think you should go to school?'

'Of course I'm going.'

And sulkily abandoning her untouched breakfast, Rowan slouched upstairs to clean her teeth, closely followed by Lady Maisie. The ghost could scarcely contain her frustration. Every time the girl began to approach the truth, she veered off into some daydream. What was this she was thinking now? Some nonsense about two lassies called Natalie and Colette—daft, outlandish names—and how she wished she could meet them after school.

It was altogether too much to bear. Gathering up her skirt in both hands, the ghost leapt from the window and allowed herself to drift down to a comfortable spot beneath some bush covered with round white flowers. Lady Maisie had paid no more heed to gardening than she had to her letters, but the flowers smelt sweet, and hopefully, if she rested here for a little, her raging spirits might be calmed. It was tiring to be always in a fury, and she had to preserve such strength as she had.

Leaning back amongst the flowers, Lady Maisie recalled her brief but exciting life. Ever since her mother's early death, Lady Maisie had ruled

Clachanfeckle like a queen, riding out with her adored father every day, and learning from him how to fight with the sgian dhu and claymore. Not that she had grown up rough and unmaidenly— on the contrary, she had been as eager to dance all night as she was to ride all day.

And now it was all gone. This very night would be the anniversary of her last hours on earth as a mortal. Exactly 252 years ago, she had climbed the twisted stair to the topmost turret of Clachanfeckle Castle, knowing that when dawn came, it would bring her death. She had taken a final look at her beloved hills and glens, and had rejoiced that, if die she must, she would die as free as she had lived.

Lady Maisie sighed deeply, and for less than a second her outline wavered into sight, just when, unfortunately, there was no-one there to see her.

Despite her great age, Lady Maisie still resembled her portrait, light brown curls held back from her lovely face with a jewelled comb, and her tartan silk dress laced tightly round her tiny waist. The white rose at her breast was as fresh as the day she had plucked it.

Then, as swiftly as it had appeared, her image faded.

Feeling herself vanish, the ghost sprang angrily to her feet. If only she could remain visible for long enough to make known her disgust at Monteith's antics! Often the anniversary of her death brought a tiny surge of power before the next, dwindling year, so tonight might be her last chance to rescue her lost honour.

Too distressed to remain reclining in the garden, Lady Maisie bounded upwards through the branches of the tree which bent gracefully over Monteith's dwelling and flung herself through the attic window. The ghost liked the attic. The dim, cobwebby space was soothing to her tired spirit. And she felt at home amongst old Mrs Monteith's possessions: the stuffed stags' heads which reminded her of hunting with her great hounds over Clachanfeckle Moor, and the paintings of Highland cattle so like the tousled beasts she had played amongst as a bairn.

Lady Maisie sank down wearily onto a tattered sofa next to a pile of books which had been thrown there. The volumes lay higgledy-piggledy, some open, some shut, some shaken free of their highly-coloured jackets. The ghost regarded them disdainfully. Books had played little part in her carefree upbringing, and even when visiting Edinburgh, she had scarcely glanced at a broadsheet or ballad, far less sat down to read. Lord Ronald, dish of whey that he was, had dearly loved to droop over a book, and these, indeed, looked exactly to his taste, with their drawings of full-bosomed hizzies.

But surely the books of her day had come in plain leather bindings? And certainly without the flaunting lassies. Lady Maisie looked more closely, spelling out the titles in their unfamiliar script. *Barefoot O'er the Heather. A Royal Fisherlassie. A Bonnie Briar Rose.* The ghost felt a cold finger of fear touch her already icy heart. She bent over one of the open volumes and began to read.

'Lady Elspeth leapt lightly from her steed into the arms of the mysterious stranger.

"I do not know your name, sir," she said, proudly withdrawing herself, "but you have the thanks of Lady Elspeth Niven. Without your aid, I would still be wandering, lost on the shores of Loch Earn."

The young man bowed gracefully, one hand on his breast. "Your servant, ma'am. They call me Murdo McLean."

"They call you Murdo McLean? So that is not your real name, sir?"

He lowered his eyes. "My real name cannot be spoken." '

What foolish words were these? Words like the evil lies she had read on the machine, but printed in a book, and that book no dreary history, but reminding her, rather, of the ballads once sold on the streets of Edinburgh. And these ballads had been bought in their dozens by highborn and lowly alike.

As the terrible truth stole over Lady Maisie, she began to keen, a heartbreaking wail quivering on the verge of audibility. 'Ochone, ochone, it is this manner of book which Monteith is writing, a book to amuse the common people, and not a morsel for a few old scholars! He is making a fool of *me*, of me, Lady Maisie of Clachanfeckle, to amuse idle women and lie-abed lassies. Och, if I could but thrust a sgian dhu into his heart, or force a quaich of poison between his teeth, or drive him mad with nightmares!'

In her anguish, the ghost generated such a strong wave of psychic power that *A Lowland Lassie* slithered off the sofa and tumbled, face down, to the floor, revealing the print on the back cover.

'Marjorie Gloaming, the best-selling novelist, whose works have been widely translated, once more delights readers all over the world with an enthralling tale of Scottish history and romance.'

Delights readers all over the world!

It had been bad enough to think that a few scholars would read Monteith's lies; this was unimaginably worse! Lady Maisie wasted no more energy on flinging books about, but crouched on the sofa, scheming. The honour of the McNeils was at stake. If she failed to silence Monteith, readers all over the world would laugh, not only at her, but at the clan which had produced the whimpering, hand-wringing maiden he had described.

So come what may, she must stop Monteith. Even if it meant that she herself faded away like a dying candle flame, the last flicker of her brave spirit consumed by the fight, she must go into battle once more, for herself, and for her clan.

At the thought of the struggle ahead, Lady Maisie's heart grew lighter. She still dearly loved a fight. Tonight she would confront her vile slanderer. Either she would ravage his machine so that every word in it was destroyed; or Monteith himself would perish.

As the ghost brooded over Robert's wickedness, she felt herself growing stronger.

'Aye, Monteith, my strength feeds on your evil! You will never escape Lady Maisie McNeil. This night will seal your doom!'

CHAPTER TEN

'Good heavens, are you actually working?'

'What does it look like?'

Rowan, who was sitting at the new pinewood desk in her bedroom window, looked coldly at her sister. She wasn't really working, work was impossible when she had so much on her mind, but she wouldn't admit it to Bryony, especially when her sister so seldom condescended to enter her room.

'You didn't used to bother. Perhaps your posh school is doing you some good after all. It would be nice if Robert's money wasn't totally wasted.'

'I only said I'd go to St Agnes's because Mum didn't want me to have that long bus ride.'

'Oh all right. I know it wasn't your fault.' Losing interest in the argument, Bryony sat down on the bed, leaning back heavily on Mr Bear.

'Don't do that!' said Rowan

instinctively.

'Oh, little pet toy bear! Oh, Mr Bear, I didn't mean to hurt you, wee Bearikins!' Bryony pulled Mr Bear out from behind her black T-shirted shoulder, and hugged him hard.

Rowan, who knew better, but couldn't stop herself, exclaimed, 'Oh don't! He can't breathe if you do that.'

'Oh, *Rowan.*'

To Rowan's surprise, Bryony put the bear down gently on the pillow. 'You're such a baby.'

'No, I'm not. And I'm working. If you're just going to lie on my bed disturbing me, you can go away.'

'OK, OK. I'd hate to interrupt the rare creative flow.' Bryony disentangled her long arms and legs and got up. As she reached the door, she turned back and said: 'By the way, what was that dream you were talking about?'

As instinctively as she'd protected Mr Bear, Rowan said, 'Don't remember.'

'Come on, Mum said you were really upset about it.'

'Why're you so worried about me all

of a sudden?'

'Well, just—' Bryony turned back into the room. The same, hesitant look which had come over her face at breakfast appeared briefly behind her makeup. 'It's just, I've been having a dream like the one Mum described. I'm following someone up a staircase, and there are more people behind me.'

'And smoke?'

'Yes.'

'And you can't see the person who's ahead of you, no matter how fast you climb?'

'Just her skirt.'

'Yes, I can see her skirt too. It's really long, but tucked up somehow.'

For the first time in weeks, the sisters looked at each other properly. Then they both jumped as the rocking chair creaked slightly.

'What was that?'

'Just the chair. It's been doing that a lot lately. I think it's the hot weather.'

Lady Maisie shook her pretty curls in disgust. The ability of mortals to find sensible reasons for hauntings infuriated her.

'Well, I don't suppose there's anything very strange in our both having the same dream,' Bryony now said, causing the ghost further annoyance. 'It's a coincidence, that's all.'

'I suppose so.' Rowan was longing to ask Bryony if she, too, woke up struggling for breath, but now that her sister had returned to being her unapproachable self, it seemed impossible.

'After all, there's only so many different dreams a person can have, right, and I expect being chased is quite a common one.'

'I expect so, but—'

'That's fine then.'

And before Rowan could say another word, Bryony had gone. Rowan sat on at her desk, staring out the window, but not seeing the picturesque view of grey sloping roofs and leafy gardens. What was happening? The haunting, if that's what it was, was spreading to Bryony. And there was only one person who could be responsible, a person who had disappeared mysteriously from this very house only three years ago. How could she find out if there had been a fire at the time?

Unable to sit still a moment longer with these horrible thoughts in her head, Rowan jumped up and ran from the room. Somehow, the house felt sinister, as though her dark thoughts had driven out the sunshine. She'd go to a call box and phone Natalie in private. Even if she couldn't bring herself to tell her friend what she suspected, it would be a comfort just to hear her voice.

Left alone, Lady Maisie was as upset and frustrated as Rowan. She had spent the day in the gloom of the attic, brooding over the revenge she would take on Monteith, and had only slipped down to Rowan's room to see if she could force the bairn to help her. But it seemed impossible to make the mortal sisters take action—or at least, action in the right direction. The elder, despite the dreams, was ignoring her, whilst the younger, as usual, was capering off on the wrong path.

She would have to act alone.

She cast her mind back 252 years to the redcoats' attack on Clachanfeckle. She had fought alone then, and tonight she would fight thus again.

CHAPTER ELEVEN

Robert was typing by the light of the full moon, which shone so brightly through his study window that it dimmed his little desk lamp. Every so often he rubbed his eyes and half-rose to close the heavy velvet curtains, only to fall back into his chair as though an invisible hand had been placed on his shoulder.

He reached for his cup of coffee, but the brew was cold and bitter, and somehow he hadn't the energy to stumble down to the kitchen to make more. His night was not going well. Usually the very act of switching on the computer and calling up his favourite work filled him with a delicious, guilty happiness, like scoffing an entire chocolate pudding, but this evening, things were going mysteriously wrong. He would type away contentedly enough, fingers flying over the keyboard—only to find that the words appearing on the screen were not those he had entered.

It was happening again! He peered in disbelief at the screen.

'Fie on you for a scurvy dish of slops, Lord Ronald! Call yourself a man, when you will not stand up and face the redcoats?' Lady Maisie kicked her suitor in the shin with the toe of her riding boot.

'D—d—don't, M—M—Maisie, I beg you,' stammered the terrified young man. 'You know I have no t—t—taste for— b—battle.'

That wasn't what he'd written. His Lady Maisie, charming, modest and sweet, would never behave in that uncouth manner, and as for Lord Ronald, he was an heroic, upstanding chap, rather as Robert imagined himself to be.

His eyes must be playing tricks on him. It was the ridiculously strong moonlight, in which the computer seemed to glow before him like a ghost machine.

Once more, Robert rose to close the curtains, and once more he collapsed back, panting, into his chair. What was wrong? Automatically, he reached for his coffee cup, but then drew back his hand, shuddering. Hadn't there once been a famous writer who had actually poisoned himself by drinking strong coffee, night after night, as he worked? Robert touched his damp brow. He was shivering with cold, yet dripping with sweat. He would leave the wretched machine until tomorrow and go to bed, where Petronella would tuck him up with a hot water bottle, as his mother used to do.

He stretched out his hand to switch off the machine—and then could not resist one last attempt to retrieve his gentle Lady Maisie. He had longed to retell her story ever since he had read it in one of his mother's old books. And what if he had altered it slightly? His Lady Maisie was a definite improvement on the original.

A sudden and extraordinarily sharp pain in his side made Robert fall forward over his desk. It was just like having a dagger thrust between his ribs. Surely not a heart attack at his age? He lay for a moment, sobbing harshly in his throat, his perspiring forehead resting on the keyboard. Then, very cautiously, he levered himself upright in his chair. He must get help. His blurred gaze fell on the screen, and another jolt of pure terror went through his body. The computer was thinking for him. The garbled text had disappeared to be replaced by the word HELP.

Robert reeled back. He was not ill but going mad.

Then, as his frantic heartbeat calmed, he realized what had happened. When his head had struck the keyboard, the machine, confused by the contradictory orders of the pressed keys, had invited him to press HELP. Of course. Now that he could see more clearly, the words on the screen were making sense.

If you need HELP, press HELP.

He would take his mechanical friend's advice. Switch off, upstairs to bed, and perhaps call the doctor in the morning if he didn't feel better. But it was probably nothing, working too hard, too much espresso late at night, too many rich meals—that wonderful tiramisu he'd made for dinner was probably the last straw!

And now the moonlight shining full on his face. No wonder people used to believe that the full moon could drive you mad.

He could almost believe it himself.

'Aye, Monteith! For once in your miserable, misbegotten life you are right!' cried Lady Maisie exultantly. She had been hovering over Robert like a vampire, growing ever stronger as her victim weakened. Now she only had to push him a little further, and he would snap, descending into madness, never to write again.

The ghost leant towards the computer, channelling her thoughts along the friendly moonbeams.

MONTEITH, YOUR TIME HAS COME! THERE IS NO ESCAPE!

Robert, dazzled, could scarcely make out the words as they appeared on the screen. He looked down at his hands, but far from moving unconsciously over the keys, they were clutching the edge of the desk.

A further message shimmered in front of him.

95

MONTEITH, I LAY THE SOLEMN SEVEN-FOLD CURSE OF THE MCNEILS UPON YOU!

Robert staggered up, knocking over his chair as he tried to reach the door. It was too late. He would never reach Petronella and safety. His beloved would find him tomorrow morning, stretched out upon the study floor, his cold face still twisted into a mask of sheer horror. Poor Petronella, what a shock it would be for her!

Lady Maisie chuckled softly. Had Robert been able to hear the eerie sound, he would undoubtedly have gone mad upon the spot.

'Och, Monteith, I do not intend your death. Quiet death is altogether too good for you. No—let your sweetheart find you the morn, but let her find a gibbering lunatic, crawling and howling like a beast upon the floor!'

Lady Maisie felt herself as triumphant and as strong as she had been on that day when she had kilted up her skirts and grasped her father's broadsword. In a moment she would be powerful enough to come into sight, thus dealing the final blow to Monteith's toppling sanity. Happier than she had ever been since her death, the ghost advanced upon the cowering author.

'Is my big bear never coming up to bed? Little bear's getting lonely.' Petronella opened the study door and peeped prettily round the edge. 'I thought I heard something fall over. Goodness me, Robert, are you all right? You look absolutely frightful.'

Robert was leaning against the bookcase, breathing in great shuddering gasps.

'Aaaaargh,' he said. And then: 'Oh, Petronella, no, I'm fine, just fine. Nothing wrong at all.'

'But you look awful!'

'No, it's just the moonlight, makes everything look odd. In fact, my eyes do hurt a bit, perhaps I need glasses.'

'It certainly is terribly bright.' Petronella tripped across the study and closed the curtains, her lace-trimmed floral nightie swishing round her little slippered feet. 'There now, isn't that better?' She pattered back to Robert and put her hand on his forehead.

'Why, you're burning hot! And yet it's so cold in here. Off to bed at once, sweetheart, you must be coming down with something.'

'I don't think so, just working too late.' Robert, still breathing hard, was getting control of himself.

'Ill or tired, what you need is a good rest.' Petronella picked up the fallen chair, and then turned to the computer. 'How do I switch this thing off?'

Robert sprang forward with a trembling cry. 'No, Petronella, don't touch it!'

'Honestly, Robert, I know you don't like people touching your things, but I only want to switch it off!'

'The screen, the screen, can you read it, what does it say?'

'Sweetheart, what *is* the matter? All it says is: "Press HELP".'

Robert made himself look at the screen. Thank God, Petronella was right. He had imagined the whole horrible thing. The mixed-up text and the final, mysterious, doom-laden message.

'Robert, there's no doubt about it,

you've definitely been working too hard. These horrid economics! Who needs another book about them anyway? Now, switch the silly thing off or close it down or whatever you call it, and then straight to bed like a good boy.'

Grasping Petronella tightly with one hand, as though to ensure his safety, Robert gingerly pressed the necessary keys. As the screen went dark, the air in the little room took on an extra chill.

'It's absolutely freezing here, it's enough to make anyone ill! And what's that funny musty smell? Could there be a dead bird stuck in the chimney? The whole place needs to be thoroughly aired.' Petronella put her arm round Robert and began to guide him lovingly towards the door. 'I know this was your mother's favourite room, but I do wish you'd let me do it up. It really does need a lick of paint.'

'Oh, do anything you like, Petronella,' said Robert wearily. 'Clean, paint, paper. I might take a break from writing for a day or two, but when I get back to work, I'm sure a new colour scheme will inspire me.'

'Oh, thank you, Robert! I'll run out and get some colour samples first thing tomorrow. And now I'll fetch you a hot water bottle and some camomile tea.'

As the young mistress's tinkling voice died away, Lady Maisie opened her lips and howled with rage and despair like one of the wolves which used to roam the hills of Clachanfeckle. Cats in the nearby gardens stopped dead, fur standing on end. Rowan and Bryony tossed in their sleep. Robert, sinking thankfully into bed, started up and seized Petronella's hand, but Petronella, stroking back his hair, only exclaimed, 'Goodness me, somebody's music is turned up loud!'

Lady Maisie howled again, but unheard. Already her strength was beginning, once more, to ebb.

Failed, failed, the one word she could bear neither to utter nor to hear!

'I cannot fail! I am a McNeil, and the McNeils never fail!'

And sobbing, her proud spirit broken at last, the ghost flung herself across Robert's desk.

CHAPTER TWELVE

'Rowan!' Once more Robert's voice was ringing down the stairs, through the sunlit hall, and into the kitchen, where Rowan and Bryony were eating cereal, while Petronella, checking through a pile of scripts, sipped her coffee. On the table between them lay a large, square parcel, addressed to Robert, which had been delivered a few moments earlier.

'Post, darling!' called Petronella, hearing her beloved's voice.

But Robert paid no attention. 'Rowan!' he called again. His voice had an unusual note in it, a note which made mother and daughters lay down their cups and spoons and, for a moment, freeze.

Then Rowan and Bryony exchanged glances and shrugs, whilst Petronella, flinging down her papers, ran out into the hall.

'Sweetheart, you're not up already, are you? Do you feel better? I thought you were going to have a long lie-in.'

Robert, who had appeared on the stairs above her, elegantly draped in his white towelling bath robe, ignored Petronella's questions, but repeated, in a terrifying, quiet roar: 'Rowan!'

Rowan, who had followed Petronella, gulped with alarm, but said as perkily as possible, 'What's the matter, Robert?'

Robert, who seemed about to repeat her name yet again, made a tremendous effort, and said, instead, 'I know you're responsible for this. This time you really have gone too far.'

Rowan tried to say, 'Responsible for what?' but her mouth was suddenly so dry that the words came out in a choked whisper. She had never actually been frightened of Robert before, but now, for some unexplained reason, he seemed so furious that she could easily imagine him picking her up and hurling her down the stairs.

'But what's happened?' Bryony had come up behind her. 'What's Rowan supposed to have done?'

'Yes, darling, what is it?' Petronella

was running up the stairs, her hands stretched out towards the white-robed figure on the landing, a figure who was shaking like a demented ghost.

'Just look at this. Just look what *your daughter*'s done now.' And Robert, seizing Petronella by the wrist, swung her round in a semi-circle until she faced the open door of his study. Petronella gave two little screams, the first of pain, the second of dismay.

'Oh Robert! I don't believe it!'

Rowan couldn't move, even when Bryony raced past her, yelling: 'Don't touch Mum!' and threw herself at Robert, kicking out with her trainers. It was the most noise Rowan had heard her make for months.

'*Bryony!*' Petronella was screaming again. 'Don't! Look!'

Robert, who had released Petronella, was now attempting to fend off Bryony, who had him backed up against the door. Black arms and legs flying, she looked like a spider about to devour a large, pallid fly.

Then, all of a sudden, Bryony stopped her attack. She had seen something over Robert's shoulder.

'Oh Robert. What happened? Do you think your computer's dead?'

Rowan finally began to climb the stairs. It seemed to take forever to raise each foot and then place it on the next step. Even when she put her hand on the banister to pull herself up, she moved with incredible slowness. And somehow she knew exactly what she was going to see when she eventually made it to the top.

Yes, she was right. The others had drawn back from the doorway at her approach, and there, in front of her, was Robert's study. Smashed. Torn apart. Blank empty spaces on the shelves where books had been pulled out and then thrown to the floor. Papers ripped into tiny jagged pieces. Edges of brightness amongst them which must be broken glass from the cabinet behind the door. And, resting on the mess of glass and paper, the computer's keyboard, which had been ripped from its socket and flung down like a dead animal. The machine itself stood alone on Robert's desk, looking forlorn without its little companion.

There was a long, long silence. Robert, Petronella and Bryony were all staring at Rowan rather than at the ruins of Robert's study.

She had to swallow several times before she could get any words out.

'It wasn't me.'

Oh, why did she sound so pathetic and childish, so *guilty*?

The silence continued around her, whilst the same icy coldness which seemed always to cling around Robert's study, swept over her, like a deadly mist.

'Of course it wasn't Rowan.' Bryony moved over to her sister and took her hand. 'Mum?' Bryony looked at Petronella, who, white as a snowdrop, was leaning against the doorway. 'Mum?'

Petronella shook her head, and looked helplessly at Robert, who, in his turn, was still standing in the corner into which Bryony had driven him.

'If it wasn't her, who was it?' he demanded. 'Petronella, you were in here last night, you saw the place when we left it. All neat and tidy, as usual.'

'Well, not quite as usual. Your chair had fallen over.'

'It didn't fall over. I knocked it over myself when I got up. Then you picked it up and I switched off the computer and the light, and we went to bed leaving everything shipshape. Well, didn't we?'

'Yes,' said Petronella reluctantly.

'Then this morning I nipped down to pick up some notes to work on in bed and . . .' Words once more failing him, Robert waved a still-trembling hand towards the wreckage.

Petronella gazed into the study, and then, sorrowfully, at Rowan. 'Oh, but darling, you wouldn't, would you? No matter how you felt?'

'*Of course* she wouldn't.' Bryony's fingers were almost mincing Rowan's, her grip was so tight.

To Rowan, her family seemed remarkably far away, their words of accusation and surprise and support distant as fairy voices. She knew what had happened in Robert's room. She knew from the chill which was invading her entire body, and from the horrible, familiar feeling of having an invisible companion at her shoulder.

'Alice did it,' she said, surprised that she could speak so calmly. 'It was Alice.'

CHAPTER THIRTEEN

'What do you mean, Alice?' said Robert hoarsely. He tried to take a step away from Rowan, but simply barged clumsily into the wall.

'Darling, you don't know what you're saying, how could it possibly be Alice?' Petronella rested her outstretched hand on Rowan's shoulder. She gave a bright, understanding smile. 'Perhaps you *do* need to speak to Mollie? Remember that dream you told me about, the one which upset you so much? Might you, just possibly, have been, well, *sleepwalking* when you, while you—?'

'The dream about the staircase!' Bryony, on Rowan's other side, still holding her hand, looked fiercely at Petronella. 'I had that dream as well, so if anyone was sleepwalking, it might just as well have been me.'

'You won't bamboozle me with all this nonsense about dreams and Alice,' said Robert, making an effort to recover his authority. 'This is sheer vandalism and I want an explanation.'

Rowan, ignoring the babble of voices around her, continued to stare at the scattered books and torn paper. Could she really have caused all this destruction in her sleep, and remained unaware of it? Impossible.

'It was Alice,' she repeated.

'Rowan, you know that can't be true. You're only making things worse—'

Bryony turned to Robert, interrupting her mother. 'Did you check if anything was stolen? It might've been a burglar.'

'Any reasonable burglar would simply have stolen the computer and cleared off!'

'Well, how about an unreasonable burglar?'

'Don't be ridiculous, Bryony!'

'Don't you two start fighting as well. As if we didn't have enough trouble—'

'Trouble, Petronella? You call the total ruin and destruction of my study, my mother's study, mere "trouble"?'

'Don't raise your voice at me, Robert Monteith!'

'Anyone at home? Oh, silly question.'

No-one noticed the clear voice, although it rang loudly up the stairwell.

'If anyone's to blame, it's really you, Robert!'

'And what exactly do you mean by that, Rowan?'

Rowan found she couldn't actually pronounce the words which were stuck in her throat. How could she say that Robert Monteith, her mother's boyfriend, the well-known economist, writer and lecturer, was also a cold-blooded murderer?

'Or perhaps I should say, *who's* at home?'

Rowan heard, and spun round.

A tall, slim young woman stood below them, her skin burnt brown by the sun and the wind, and her very short hair bleached white. She was wearing loose trousers tucked into high leather boots and a striped poncho.

Instinctively, Rowan turned back to see Robert's face, and then wished that she hadn't. He looked exactly like a horrible dead fish, eyes glazed and mouth hanging open. His skin had gone an awful grey colour.

'Don't worry, darling, I'm not a ghost,' said the woman merrily, starting up the stairs.

Robert was making curious gulping noises. 'Alice. Alice,' he brought out at last. 'Why didn't you write? I thought you were dead.'

And so did I, thought Rowan, who knew that she must look as astonished as Robert. Although astonished was hardly the word for what she felt. Flabbergasted. Overwhelmed. Flabberwhelmed, even. And relieved. Robert had shrunk back into being Mum's irritating boyfriend, and her feeling of being haunted by an angry ghost must be sheer imagination.

But in that case, *who had trashed the study*?

'Oh, Robert, and I didn't think you cared! I did try to send you the odd card, but there's not much in the way of a postal service on the altiplano.'

'But I'd no idea where you *were*!' Robert's voice rose to a pathetic squeak.

'Honestly, Robert, my note couldn't have made things clearer! "Gone to

111

climb the Andes with Nico." '

'But I was *worried* about you!'

'What nonsense, who would worry about me!' And stopping halfway up the stairs, Alice put her hands on her hips and laughed. She had a mouthful of huge square teeth. 'I can look after myself.'

Too true, thought Rowan. She had never met anyone who seemed as well able to take care of herself as Alice. She was as tall as Robert, but with all the authority and swagger which he lacked. She could have been a gypsy or a pirate or a bandit queen. As she came nearer, Rowan could actually smell her, a scent of herbs and smoke and something meaty. Or perhaps, judging by her grubby fingernails, Alice hadn't washed very thoroughly since her return to civilization.

As his wife advanced, Robert retreated, fluttering his hands helplessly. 'Alice, I just can't believe it's you.'

'Alive and kicking.'

'But excuse me, you don't live here any more. Just where do you think you're going?'

Rowan couldn't imagine how her mother dared address Alice, the warrior queen like this, but in defence of Robert and her beloved ruffled curtains and bowls of pot-pourri and matching sheets and pillow cases, Petronella stepped bravely in front of her.

'We haven't been introduced.' Alice, towering over Petronella, held out her big brown hand. 'Alice Monteith. I dare say you've heard all about me but I don't know a thing about you.'

Petronella, hypnotized by the gleaming eyes and grinning wolf teeth, shook hands. 'Petronella Durwood.'

'And?' Alice made a large gesture towards the still-thunderstruck Bryony and Rowan.

'Oh. My daughters. Bryony. Rowan.'

Rowan had a ridiculous urge to curtsey.

'Pretty girls. Well, Robert, you have taken on a handful, haven't you?'

Robert made some more gulping noises.

'Don't worry, Petronella,' continued

Alice, still smiling. 'I haven't come to stay. I just want the stuff I left in the attic. I hope you haven't thrown it all out. I see you've made quite a lot of changes.' She looked appreciatively at the new wallpaper, sprigged with tiny pink flowers. 'Nice.'

'The boxes in the attic?' said Petronella, rubbing life back into the hand which Alice had squeezed. 'Oh no, I didn't touch anything. In case you ever came back for them.'

'Excellent. I see you've got more sense than Robert. Wouldn't be difficult, of course. I'll just nip up and get what I want, then I'll be on my way. Nico's going to pick me up in half an hour. We're off to Mongolia next week. My God, Robert, what's happened to your study?'

Alice, striding on towards the upper staircase, had finally come in sight of the wreckage.

No-one answered.

Oh no, thought Rowan. I said *Alice* had done it. I meant Alice's *ghost*, but now the others will think I meant *this* Alice.

'We don't know,' she said quickly. 'When Robert went in this morning, he just found it. Like this.'

'The poltergeist,' said Alice airily. 'Fancy it still hanging around.'

'What do you mean, Alice?'

'Poltergeist?'

'What *is* a poltergeist?'

Everyone was staring at Alice.

'Just a silly little mischievous spirit,' she said. 'You have to be firm with them.'

As she spoke, the heavy velvet curtains on the study window tugged slightly at their rings, and then, fold by fold, slipped off the rail and fell to the ground.

'What did I tell you?' said Alice. 'It used to try and tease me when I lived here, but I wouldn't stand any nonsense from it. You've obviously let it get out of hand, Robert. Now, Petronella, do you have any plastic bags I could have? I'll just stuff a few things into them, and then I'll be off.'

'In the kitchen,' said Petronella faintly.

'Fetch them for me, there's a

sweetie, I wouldn't know where to look. The kitchen was never my department.' And Alice strode up the stairs, her poncho rippling around her.

As she passed him, Robert stumbled backwards into the safety of his study, slamming the door behind him. He obviously preferred the company of a poltergeist to that of his wife.

Petronella and the girls were left on the half-landing, gaping at one another.

'It wasn't Rowan,' said Bryony, finally. 'It was a poltergeist. We all saw it, didn't we, Mum?'

'Yes, it actually was a poltergeist.' Rowan sat down on the stairs. She had been proved innocent by something which she hadn't even known existed. Then she noticed, as she smoothed her skirt down over her trembling knees, what she was wearing. School uniform.

'We ought to have been at school *hours* ago!'

'Don't worry about school, darling. I'll phone.'

'You can hardly tell them we're not there because we've been haunted.'

'I'll think of something. I am an

actress.' Petronella hovered uncertainly, one hand on the banister. She couldn't quite meet Rowan's eye. 'Sorry, darling,' she said. Then she turned and ran downstairs.

'She really thought I'd done it,' said Rowan, once the kitchen door had shut behind her mother.

'And that's the most she'll ever say about it,' said Bryony, sitting down beside her sister. 'In fact, you're lucky she's even sort of apologized.'

'But the way the curtain just slid off the rail like that. It couldn't have been, oh, an earthquake, could it, or perhaps the rail was broken and it suddenly gave way—?'

'It was a poltergeist,' said Bryony, with conviction. 'It happened so slowly.'

'And if Alice hadn't turned up, we'd never have known. Robert would have gone on blaming me. And so would Mum.'

They sat in silence for a bit. Then Bryony said: 'Why did you say that Alice had done it?'

Rowan thought quickly. 'Oh, I

117

suspected she might have come back secretly and smashed things up because she was angry with Robert.'

Bryony thought about it. 'You know, that's quite a logical idea. I'm surprised none of us thought of that.'

'Well, thank you very much.'

'And all the time it was something so *illogical* we'd never have dreamt of it.'

'Bryony?'

'Yeah?'

'Do you think it was the poltergeist giving us that dream? About being chased and everything?'

'Don't know.'

Bryony seemed to be returning to her old silent self. Rowan wished she could make her speak to her properly again.

'Do you think Robert will be any different now he's seen Alice again?'

'How would I know?'

'Do you think—'

'I don't *know*.'

'One of you take these up to *Mrs Monteith.*' And Petronella, appearing at the foot of the stairs, tossed a pile of poly bags onto the floor.

CHAPTER FOURTEEN

'The nerve of it! Calling *me* a poltergeist—an aristocratic phantom like myself!'

Lady Maisie lay, worn out with anger and despair, on the attic sofa, while Alice, unaware of her baleful companion, cheerfully stuffed jerseys, socks and woolly vests into the bags which Bryony had brought up to her.

The ghost was finally at her wits' end. After Robert and Petronella's departure the previous night, she had attempted to destroy the mechanical beast, but when it proved too heavy to hurl to the floor, she had flown into a childish tantrum and tossed and torn and ripped apart anything her feeble hand could lift.

Then, so exhausted that she faded from even her own awareness, Lady Maisie had collapsed on top of the broken glass. And there she had lain until roused by that vile taunt 'poltergeist', uttered in the tones of her old enemy, Mistress Alice Monteith, who, far from being dead, was most horribly alive. The ghost had surged up from the floor through the ceiling to the attic, dislodging, as she did so, the curtains whose pole she had already broken in her furious rampage.

But this last leap had been her undoing.

Now completely spent, Lady Maisie could only watch as Alice, humming softly to herself, sat back on her heels and surveyed the attic. Her gaze travelled over the stags' heads, the painted cattle, and for obvious reasons, through Lady Maisie. But something on the once-elegant old sofa caught her eye. The pile of Marjorie Gloamings. Alice, rising to her feet, gave a whoop of amusement and delight.

When the terrible woman had finally gone, taking her bags of disgusting, grubby clothing with her, Lady Maisie allowed herself to shed a solitary tear. Soon, indeed, readers all over the world would mock her as Alice had just mocked the Marjorie Gloamings. The book which she had failed to prevent

Monteith from writing was just another such ridiculous romance. And now she was so weak that it could not be long before she flickered out and vanished, just as the moonbeams had vanished when Petronella pulled the curtain.

The ghost's hand wandered to the white rose on her breast.

'Ochone, my prince,' she moaned. 'I have failed my clan. I will not be worthy to join you. Farewell, Prince Charles Edward Stuart.'

*   *   *

'I see you put all those awful Marjorie Gloamings in the attic. Well done, you. I would never have dared.'

Alice had appeared in the kitchen doorway, her poncho fringed with dust and cobwebs.

Petronella, Bryony and Rowan all looked up cautiously. Petronella and Bryony were drinking very strong coffee, and Rowan, hot chocolate. They were all eating shortbread biscuits. Robert was still hiding in his study. Petronella had taken him up a tray, but he had snatched it from her at the door without a word. Now the mother and daughters were attempting to recover, after the astonishing events of the morning, with the aid of caffeine and sugar.

'Those wretched books were the bane of my life,' Alice continued cheerfully. 'Any chance of a spot of coffee? Nico won't be here for at least ten minutes.'

'Black? White? Sugar? A mug or a cup?' Petronella, transformed by the request into a hostess, fluttered around the table, while Alice sat down as though she had never been away.

'I simply didn't dare get rid of them.' Alice stirred heaped spoonfuls of sugar into her coffee.

'I didn't want that sentimental trash lying around for the girls to get hold of,' said Petronella.

'I hope you didn't say that to Robert. He was frightfully proud of his mum's work.'

'I beg your pardon?' Petronella sank back into her chair. 'What did you say?'

'You mean you didn't know? Robert

never told you?' Alice's face was shining with mischief. 'You didn't know that Mrs Monteith was Marjorie Gloaming?'

Petronella stared back at her, pale and speechless.

'You mean Robert's mother wrote all those daft books which Mum put in the attic?' said Bryony.

'No wonder he was angry!' said Rowan.

And the two girls began to giggle hysterically.

Alice joined in with a hearty bellow. 'I wish I'd seen his face! I was terrified to touch the beastly things, and then you put them in the attic! Well, it says a lot for his devotion that he forgave you, Petronella. I'm glad I'm leaving him in such good hands because, when all's said and done, he *is* quite a sweetie, isn't he?'

As Alice ended her speech, the doorbell rang.

'Nico, bless him, dead on time. Why do Italians have this ridiculous reputation for unpunctuality? Well, I'll be off.' Alice swallowed the last of her coffee, and jumping to her feet, picked up her bags. 'Give Robert my love, won't you, Pet, and tell him to get a move on with the divorce, if he hasn't started already. Goodbye, girls, lovely to meet you, I'll try and send you a postcard but God knows what the post's like in Mongolia, Outer far less Inner.'

And Alice disappeared, marching heartily down the hall, and then slamming the front door behind her.

CHAPTER FIFTEEN

Complete silence settled upon the kitchen. Rowan and Bryony stopped giggling and looked apologetically at Petronella, who still hadn't said a word. Then she lifted her hands helplessly and let them fall back into her lap.

'Oh Robert!' she cried. 'What have I done?'

'So all those Scottish books in Robert's study *did* belong to his mother,' said Rowan.

'What books?'

'Oh Bryony, he's got a whole cupboard of history books and stuff. But he said he *didn't* have them. Perhaps he didn't want us to guess that his mother wrote romantic novels.'

'And I made fun of Marjorie Gloaming!' moaned Petronella. 'I said her writing was a . . . was a tartan travesty of real art!' She looked as though she were about to cry. 'I don't suppose he's really forgiven me, not in his heart.'

'Oh Petronella, how could anyone not forgive you?'

Robert had come down the stairs soundlessly in his soft leather slippers. He was still wearing his dressing-gown, and his hair was thoroughly tousled, as though he had been tugging at it with both hands. 'I should have told you that Mother was Marjorie Gloaming, but she always kept it a secret. I dare say Alice let the cat out of the bag. She has gone, hasn't she?' He looked around warily.

'You told Alice and not me!'

'No, Mother told Alice herself. She thought Alice ought to know the family secret because she was going to marry me. And I would have told you, Petronella, I mean, it's nothing to be ashamed of, I would've told you, but well, but—'

'I know!' broke in Petronella, 'it's all my own fault. I never gave you a chance. I made fun of Marjorie Gloaming!' And covering her face with her hands, she burst into loud wailing sobs.

Rowan and Bryony looked at one

another. They had heard the pitiful sound many times before. Robert, however, rushed to Petronella's side and gently put his arms around her.

'No, no, darling, it was all *my* fault! I should have told you right away—I'm to blame. Please, Petronella, don't cry, you're breaking my heart.'

Rowan almost felt a twinge of sympathy for Robert in her own heart.

'Oh, Mum,' she said briskly. 'Stop making such a fuss. All you've got to do is say "sorry" to Robert.' She stopped abruptly. Was it only three days ago that Mum had been telling *her* to say sorry to Robert after he'd accused her of disturbing his notes? Of course, that must've been the poltergeist too!

'Rowan's right,' said Bryony firmly. 'No-one's blaming you for laughing at Marjorie Gloaming, Mum. After all, even Robert's got to admit that no-one reads her these days.'

'Well, that's where you're mistaken.' Releasing Petronella, Robert picked up the parcel which had been lying on the table, forgotten since its delivery a couple of hours earlier. He began to tear at the wrapping. 'If this is what I think it is—'

'But *what* is it, Robert?' said Petronella almost timidly, raising her beautiful tear-drenched face. She never went red or blotchy when she cried.

'Here.' Bryony handed Robert the kitchen scissors. Wielding them, he sliced swiftly through tape and brown paper to reveal a stack of brand new books, each in a colourful jacket.

Robert snatched one of them and held it aloft. 'So what do you say to that?'

'It's just a book,' said Rowan blankly. Obviously the destruction of his study and the amazing return of his wife had driven Robert out of his mind. It was hardly surprising.

'Oh no. Oh look,' said Bryony.

Rowan looked. 'Oh no,' she repeated. She was the one who was going mad. 'But she's dead. Your mother *is* dead, isn't she, Robert?'

'What do you mean, girls? Robert? What's the matter?' Petronella looked from one to another, her tears finally quenched. 'Who's dead?'

'My poor mama is dead, but Marjorie Gloaming lives on!' cried Robert triumphantly. He waved the book in their astonished faces. 'Advance copies of the latest Marjorie Gloaming: "*A Scots Bluebell*—a tender tale of intrigue and romance—awaited eagerly by her faithful readers".'

He laid the glossy volume respectfully on the table. The cover showed a beautiful young woman in a low-cut tartan bodice, posed becomingly against a blue mountainside.

'But how can she have faithful readers if she's *dead*?'

'Oh, Mum, it's easy,' said Bryony scornfully. 'Someone else is writing them, using her name. I expect some hack in the publishing company turns them out.'

Robert's flushed face darkened.

'No,' said Rowan slowly. 'No.' She remembered Robert's study the night she had crept in, the books on costume and history across the desk, the snatch of a story which she had caught on the screen. 'Robert's writing them now, aren't you, Robert? You're Marjorie

Gloaming.'

'Yes,' he said. He was looking both exhausted and pleased with himself, as though he'd just run a marathon. 'Oh, Petronella, I've been wanting to tell you so badly, but I thought you'd laugh. However, now the secret's out, I don't care anymore. Make fun of me as much as you like, but I'm proud of being Marjorie.'

No-one even sniggered. There was something about the strangely noble look on Robert's face which made laughter quite impossible.

'So you're actually your mother's ghost writer,' said Bryony, after several long seconds of respectful silence. 'You're writing, pretending to be her.'

'Yes,' he said, 'I suppose I am. You see, when my mother died, she had left her last book, *A Royal Fisherlassie*, almost complete, so her publisher suggested that they find someone to finish it. However, when I looked at her notes, they were so detailed that I was able to follow them and finish it myself. Then I found all the notes for her next book—*Barefoot O'er the*

130

Heather—so I just thought I'd try my hand at that, and one thing led to another . . . I've actually been Marjorie for three years now, ever since Alice left.'

'So Alice didn't know that you'd taken over where your mother left off?' said Petronella.

'Oh no. Writing Marjorie's books kept me busy in the lonely evenings. Until I met you, Petronella.' He took her hand.

'So how did you know, Rowan, if it was such a secret?' said Bryony.

'Because I went into Robert's room one night and saw all those books on Scottish history and stuff on his desk, didn't I, Robert?'

'But you said you didn't have any history books!' exclaimed Petronella. 'You lied to me, Robert!' Her face was starting to crumple again into tearful folds.

'I know I shouldn't have lied, but I didn't want anyone to see the books and guess. Like Rowan did, in fact.' He glared briefly at Rowan over Petronella's bent head.

'I don't blame you, Robert,' said Bryony. 'If I were Marjorie Gloaming, I'd keep it a total secret.'

'Me too,' said Rowan. 'I'd let myself be bitten to death by vampires before I'd tell.'

'I've said I'm not ashamed,' said Robert, his eyes on Petronella. 'It was just—oh, Petronella—I was afraid you wouldn't *respect* me if you knew.'

'Robert, I could never cease to respect you,' said Petronella, speaking very slowly and seriously. 'But what I don't understand is, why are you still writing them? You're not alone any more.' And she raised her free hand to smooth his tangled hair.

Robert returned her gaze frankly. 'Money,' he said.

'What?' said Rowan and Bryony together.

'I only teach part-time, and my serious books don't bring in much. It's Marjorie who paid for my Volvo and for your clarsach, Bryony, and Rowan's school fees—and even that dress you're wearing, Petronella.'

'So Marjorie's a nice little earner?'

said Bryony.

'Yes, you could call her that, but I enjoy it. It's such a change from writing about politics and statistics. One moment, I'm galloping across the heather with gallant Lord Ronald, and the next I'm besieged in her castle with beautiful Lady Maisie McNeil—'

'With—who did you say?'

'Lady Maisie McNeil of Clachanfeckle, the heroine of my latest book, *The Lassie Wi' the White Rose*. Young, lovely, in deadly peril until she's rescued by her sweetheart, Lord Ronald. It's based on a true story.'

'But that wasn't what really happened!' Rowan hadn't meant to scream, but somehow the words were torn out of her. She was also feeling, all of a sudden, the old deadly chill creeping over her.

CHAPTER SIXTEEN

Lady Maisie had faltered down from the attic, drawn by Rowan's wild cry, and was now lying, full length, along the top of the dresser. Despite herself, she felt a flicker of hope. Perhaps the bairn would save her after all?

'Rowan! Don't shout at Robert like that!'

'But she's right, Petronella!' Robert had whirled round towards Rowan. 'How did you know that?'

Rowan shook her head hopelessly. She had no idea where her speech had come from. She only knew that she could, yet again, smell smoke, and her ears were full of the sound of dashing steel. Someone was screaming over the hubbub, not with fear, but with a wild note of defiance: 'I will die before I surrender my castle! If Clachanfeckle falls, then I fall with it!'

'Rowan, darling, what's wrong? You've gone terribly white.' Petronella came anxiously towards her.

Rowan, who had leapt up, sat down shakily at the table and put her head in her hands. 'I don't know,' she said, 'I don't know how I'm so sure, but Lord Ronald didn't rescue Lady Maisie. He ran away, and she died defending the castle.'

Robert was staring at her, his face frozen with astonishment. 'But that *is* what really happened! How on earth could you have found out?'

'I must've read it somewhere.' She knew that wasn't the truth, but it seemed the only explanation which the adults would accept.

'I do have a book about the siege in my study—'

'Then I expect I must've looked at it that night I went in. Sorry, Robert.'

But it was Bryony whose eyes she met, and she knew that her sister didn't believe her.

'Well, that explains it,' said Robert. 'No more poltergeists or dreams, eh? Yes, most of the men of Clachanfeckle had gone with Lady Maisie's father to fight for Prince Charlie, but when the English attacked the castle, she rallied the old men and boys and fought for as long as she could. Then, when she realized that there was no hope of rescue, she set fire to the castle rather than surrender.'

'You mean she was burnt to death?' Rowan had to ask, although she could hardly bear to hear the answer.

'No, in the confusion an English officer ran her through with his sword. She had her skirt tucked up so that she could fight, and, blinded by the smoke, he thought she was a kilted clansman. And killed her.'

Rowan gave a deep, deep sigh. The smoke was clearing, and through the last wisps she could see the beautiful young woman whose portrait she had admired in Robert's study, lying on a staircase, the white rose on her breast red with blood. Bending over her was a handsome soldier, his stained sword in his hand. Tears were running down his cheeks.

High on the dresser, Lady Maisie was also weeping, the drops falling unseen onto Petronella's shopping list.

'What happened to the officer?'

'Nobody knows. Apparently he was so horrified by what he'd done that he gave up the army. Then he disappears from sight, like most people in history. It's only a few exceptional characters, like Lady Maisie, who are remembered.'

' "An exceptional character",' sobbed the ghost.

'Oh, that's such a sad story!' cried Petronella, giving a sigh of her own.

'Yes, that's why I'm only using it as a basis for my book. Marjorie's readers wouldn't like it if the heroine got killed off.'

'But that's unfair!' Rowan slammed both palms flat on the table. 'It's unfair to—to Lady Maisie's memory! Your book makes it sound as though she were sitting round meekly, waiting to be rescued, when really she was ready to die for her freedom.'

'Rowan's right!' said Bryony. Her usually pale face was blazing. 'You can't write a lie like that about a real person. Think how brave she must've been, setting fire to the castle, when she knew it meant her own death!'

'Och, I *was* brave,' echoed the ghost, eyes glowing with an almost visible light.

'But there is a difference between Art and Life,' said Robert patronizingly. 'The writer has to ask himself the question: "Does it make a good story?" '

'Well, I think, in this case, the truth makes a better story,' said Petronella unexpectedly. 'The real Lady Maisie behaved just like one of Shakespeare's heroines, valiant, feisty, afraid of nothing.'

Lady Maisie was now sitting up and crooning with delight. 'Aye, afraid of nothing! At last, Monteith, the truth is out!'

'Yes, Robert, the real story would make a great book!' said Rowan eagerly.

'No-one wants to read about soppy heroines nowadays,' said Bryony.

'Give today's women positive role models,' said Petronella.

'Like Alice,' said Rowan. 'I bet Lady Maisie was just like Alice.'

Robert shuddered. The last thing he wanted was to write about someone like Alice. 'You don't understand,' he said. 'In this type of book—'

'Then write a *different* type of book,' snapped Bryony.

'Yeah, you could write a *serious* historical novel, but under a different name—'

'You don't have to be Marjorie all your life.'

'Or you could *begin* the book with Maisie's brave death, and then write about the officer who killed her, and you could imagine what happened to him when he left the army—'

'Yes!' put in Petronella. 'He wanders around Europe, stricken by remorse—'

'He searches out Maisie's lovely young cousin, to make amends,' said Rowan.

'And falls in love with her—' said Bryony.

'She loves him back, but family honour forbids her marrying the man who killed her cousin—'

'But in the end she relents and then they run away to America together to start a new life—'

'And finally they have a baby

daughter and call her Maisie!'

The two girls burst out laughing, whilst the ghost joined in with a peal of unearthly glee.

'Nimbly done, lassies! Ach, you are not so daft after all!' Bolt upright now, her white face enlivened by the least tinge of pink, the ghost looked as beautiful as she had been on the day the English sword pierced her heart.

'Oh that's wonderful!' cried Petronella. 'Robert, that would make a much better book, and it wouldn't be untrue to Lady Maisie's memory. You said yourself that no-one knew what had happened to the soldier, so it wouldn't matter if you made up something about him.'

'Yes,' said Rowan. 'Your hero will be inspired by Lady Maisie's bravery.'

'That's all very well,' said Robert, 'but I've already started *The Lassie Wi' the White Rose* and—'

'But just because you've started doesn't mean you have to finish,' said Bryony.

'Oh, Robert, it would be so *noble* to give up writing a book which none of us liked!' Petronella clasped her hands under her chin in the gesture she'd used when playing Juliet.

'Oh yes, Robert, please be fair to Lady Maisie!' Rowan realized, as she spoke, that never before had she asked Robert for anything.

Robert stood at bay, fixed by three pairs of pleading eyes. Naturally, he could never resist Petronella, but it was unsettling to have both Bryony and Rowan looking at him like that. As though he could actually, at last, do something to please them.

'If it really means so much to all of you . . .' They were watching him, he thought, like three puppies eager for a meal or a walk. But puppies who could deliver a sharp little bite if they didn't get what they wanted. 'I'll change it. It'll mean quite a bit of extra work, and I'll have to ditch at least a hundred pages, but it would be quite challenging to start with a tragic death, and then move on to the love story—'

Lady Maisie leapt from the dresser and began to dance triumphantly in mid-air, bounding over the sunbeams as though they were the crossed blades of the Highland Sword Dance.

Petronella also sprang to her feet and flung herself on Robert, winding her arms round him. 'Oh, Robert, thank you! I know you can do it! I'm so proud of you.'

Rowan and Bryony watched the scene with their usual disgust, but couldn't help grins from spreading over their faces. Bryony shrugged and made for the door, but turning at the last minute, said: 'If you want to make the cousin musical, Robert, I could give you some advice about the tunes she might play.'

Robert actually stopped embracing Petronella in order to look at her daughter. 'Thank you very much, Bryony, I'd appreciate that.'

'OK then.' As Bryony disappeared upstairs, Rowan realized, inevitably, that it was her turn to say something nice.

'I think you're doing the right thing, Robert,' she said stiffly.

'And thank you too, Rowan.' Robert's face was absolutely glowing with self-satisfaction. His sacrifice had been worthwhile.

'And I'm going to do the right thing as well!' Releasing Robert, Petronella skipped out into the hall. 'I'm going up to the attic this very minute, and I'm going to bring down all the Marjorie Gloamings and put them straight back into the drawing room. In pride of place.'

'Oh, sweetheart, thank you. I'll come and help.'

'No, no, you run along and tidy your study. You'll have to clear up before you can start the new book.'

'There's plenty of time for that. It's not as bad as it looks. At least the computer's OK, and the keyboard seems to have survived the fall. So I insist on escorting you to the attic. I'll protect you from the spiders.'

'As though I'd be frightened of a spider!'

Rowan sighed yet again as the couple departed up the staircase, bickering lovingly. She supposed she didn't have any choice except to bear it—especially since Alice had just disappeared into the Mongolian sunset. Perhaps, when Rowan was a bit older, Alice might take her along on her travels. Or she could always go off on adventures of her own. She imagined trekking across the desert, or exploring the Atlas mountains . . .

'You're not still sitting here, are you?' Bryony had come back into the room. 'Are you all right? You look a bit peculiar.'

Rowan shook herself. She had no idea for how long she'd been daydreaming. She said quickly, 'I just can't believe how much has happened in one morning. I think it's made me a bit dizzy. The poltergeist, Alice, Robert being Marjorie Gloaming—' She took in Bryony's appearance, the old rucksack which had once been their father's over her shoulder, fresh black make-up round her eyes. 'You're not going to school, are you?'

'Why not? Just because I've missed most of the morning, it doesn't mean I've got to miss the afternoon as well.'

'I don't think I could bear to go. The house feels so warm and peaceful, somehow. It's nice just sitting here.'

'Rowan.' Bryony rested her bag for a moment on the table. 'Rowan, how did you know what really happened to Lady Maisie? You didn't read it, did you?'

Rowan looked up at her sister. 'I don't know,' she said. 'I mean, Robert does have a book, but it doesn't give any details. I just seemed to see it all somehow.'

'Like in the dream?'

'Yes.' Their eyes met across the empty coffee cups and the stack of Marjorie Gloamings. 'But it's gone now.'

'The smoke?'

'Yes. And—you know, whoever was there.'

Bryony hesitated for a moment. Then she swung her bag onto her shoulder. 'I'd better go, or I'll be late for maths. See you.'

'Yeah, see you.'

And, without looking back, Bryony disappeared.

Rowan sat on at the table, gazing after her sister. Perhaps Bryony would come travelling with her? She could bring her clarsach and play at night to the nomads whom they met on their way.

They would go somewhere hot. Rowan loved being warm, as she was at this moment. The sun had moved round to shine full in the kitchen window, and the whole room smelt of the little white roses which Petronella had arranged in a bowl in the middle of the table.

Poor Lady Maisie. They had been her flower, the symbol of her devotion to Prince Charles Edward Stuart, but at least now, in Robert's new book, her true bravery would shine out like—like the sunlight on all the plates and dishes on the dresser.

As Rowan watched, all the separate sparkles seemed, for an instant, to run into one glowing column which centred itself upon the bowl of roses. It hovered there, lighting up the flowers, the pots of herbs, the frilly curtains, Rowan herself, and then, as swiftly and mysteriously as it had appeared, it was gone.